*ZACH KRYTON*
*THRILLER*

# PHOENIX

## JOSH
## FRANCIS

Phoenix – The Zach Kryton Introductory Series Book 3

This is the sequel to Pegasus and Poseidon – it is recommended you read them both first

WARNING: some obscene language

Josh Francis

ISBN: 9-780648-702528 (paperback)

Published by Red Diamond
www.red-diamond.com.au/books

Sign up to the reader's group

This story is fictional!

Cover media by Onur Aksoy – Great work Onur!
www.onegraphica.com

# Also By Josh Francis

*Pegasus* – The Zach Kryton Introductory Series (Book 1).

*Poseidon* – The Zach Kryton Introductory Series (Book 2).

*Phoenix* – The Zach Kryton Introductory Series (Book 3).

*Battle Rhythm* – The military-inspired personal planning, discipline and motivation guide (The Camouflage Series Book 1).

*Centre of Gravity* – The principles soldiers use to think, act and achieve success (The Camouflage Series Book 2).

*Under the Pump* – Anecdotes of a service station operator.

# Follow Us

You can find other publications and join our conversations on social media. This will keep you up to date with upcoming books and allow you to share ideas. Feel free to contribute!

INSTAGRAM

FACEBOOK

AMAZON

Please leave an honest review on Amazon. This helps to tailor and improve the content of what we produce.

# Contents

# 1

The wailing sound of sirens filled the night sky as rain drizzled slowly onto the streets. The occasional lightning flash in the distance indicated that the evening storm was moving away from the national capital.

People stood around as the emergency services entered the building, responding to the fire alarm on level 50 which had forced the building to be evacuated.

In actuality, it was a ploy initiated by the Ministry of State Security – the MSS – to hide the incident that involved shots being fired during the high-level diplomatic function.

Zach Kryton sat on the edge of the back of an ambulance as a paramedic helped apply some ointment to the various cuts on his face. Fortunately, his nose wasn't broken. The young paramedic then gave the Australian operator an ice pack for his knee, which Kryton applied over his bruised joint. He grimaced as the cool ice touched his exposed knee, but it soon felt soothing, helping to numb the pain. His entire body ached, as would be expected after having been in two fights in the same night.

Kryton nodded at the paramedic, who smiled as he moved away to help the other injured people caught up in the stampede in the function centre.

He looked up. Agent Chen of the MSS looked back at him, sympathetically. Her presence was comforting to Kryton – if not least because she had saved his life.

"So," he said, "to whom do I owe my gratitude?"

She smiled.

"I'm Yiling Chen. I'm head of security for the Chinese cultural mission here in Taipei."

Kryton looked at her disbelievingly.

"Is that a fancy way of saying that you're Head of Station for the MSS?" he asked, referring to the term used for the head spy in any given country.

She softly tilted her head. She stepped in closer to him, seeking to avoid the alert ears of any eavesdroppers.

"Well, China does not officially have diplomatic relations with Taiwan," she said.

"And why is that?"

"Officially, Taiwan is part of China. Why would we have diplomatic relations with our own province!?" she asked rhetorically.

Kryton smiled and nodded as he pulled the radio from his hip, an action that hurt more than he thought it would. It was all smashed up. That would explain why he had lost communications with Guam a while ago after the fight with Wallis.

"You're still using the older model!?" said Agent Chen wryly.

He couldn't help but laugh, which hurt his bruised ribs.

"We make do with what we have," he replied.

Kryton sat upright as a well-dressed man approached Chen, whispering something in Mandarin in her ear.

Kryton looked around. The crowd had started to disperse as firefighters left the building, replaced by a horde of police officers trying to determine what had actually happened. He gave himself a quick examination, but was confident that he had no significant injuries.

Chen finished her conversation and looked back at Kryton. He breathed in deeply, now focusing on what was to happen next.

"How did you know I was here?" he asked firmly.

She nodded knowingly and understood that an explanation would ease his wariness of her.

"A few days ago, our navy attacked a small outpost in the South China Sea."

"Oh?" he said, feigning any knowledge of said attack which had almost killed him.

She smiled as she sat down next to him on the back of the ambulance.

"It's okay. We know you were there."

He looked at her, a tinge of anger in his eyes. He wanted to know why they had shelled his team. She sensed his building fury.

"Since the attack on Air Force One in Dili, our governments have still maintained some lines of communication through fairly well-established back channels."

2

He nodded, knowing full well the practice occurred – even amongst enemies during time of war.

"We received warning from a source in the local emergency services that there might be an attempted bombing at the reception tonight," she said, gesturing at the 101 building.

Kryton thought for a moment. Any analyst worth their salt knew that that information alone wouldn't mean much. He was confident in his cover profile. She must have known more.

"But how do you know my name?"

"We reached out to the Americans, trying to find out what they might know about any potential attack. We reached out through these channels. They informed us that you were trying to stop an attack in the 101 building, and that you might need some help. They told us that you had been following a lead that had taken you to the same outpost we attacked."

"So, if they shared that information with you, obviously my side no longer thinks that it was your people who attacked the U.S. President."

Chen nodded before continuing.

"Yes. So that's how we found out about you."

"In that case, I imagine that, like us, you've also been trying to find out who is responsible for the attack in Dili," he said.

"Exactly. We don't want war any more than you do. We attacked the outpost on the island after an anonymous source provided us with very reliable intelligence that showed that there was a rogue PLA element on there who conducted the attack on the U.S. President. We've also been chasing a stolen PLA submarine that we know has been used to deliver arms into Timor."

Kryton listened closely to all that she was saying. It was obvious that both sides had various pieces of intelligence. They were now in a position to start putting those pieces together. He was quickly warming to her. It was rare for a Chinese official to so freely admit to something that made the Chinese government lose face – such as losing an operational submarine.

He noticed that she was young and attractive. A little too young to be running a spy station, though. This meant one of two things: either she was a star performer, or her relatives had high positions in the Central Committee of the Communist Party.

She wouldn't be in her role any other way.

"Our investigations indicate that some rogue elements in the PLA are part of a wider conspiracy."

Kryton nodded while sighing. This was a lot of information, and he realised it was probably pure luck that his team had made it off of Zulu One alive.

He rubbed his knee.

"Well, I'm glad you arrived when you did?" he said.

The paramedic returned to check on Kryton. He told the young man that he was alright. Chen then guided Kryton away from the ambulance and over to a quieter area near the side of the building. A small team of fit-looking men in dark suits provided a small cordon around Agent Chen.

It was her bodyguard detail. Their presence made it obvious that she was an important person.

"Did you know about the outpost on the island before your anonymous source tipped you off? Such as through signals intercepts of other ways?" asked Kryton.

"No. We've been chasing a series of communications from various phones and satellites associated with the submarine and our missing PLA members, but it was actually just lucky that we found out. We didn't believe the Americans knew about the outpost, so we attacked it. We were trying to resolve an internal issue. I'm sorry if anyone in your team got hurt."

"It's okay. If anything, it might have convinced my side that you weren't the perpetrators of the Dili attack."

Kryton looked closely at her. She seemed sincere, but he was trained to always err on the side of caution and not to share too much information unnecessarily.

*If the Chinese were tipped off, it means that either Wallis has a leak, or we do,* he thought to himself, knowing that if the Chinese didn't know about the outpost on the island or the attack on the function through other means, then their sources had to have been told either by someone in Wallis's camp, or the American one.

"If you're talking to my people, can you get me in touch with them?" he asked her.

Chen said something to one of the bodyguards in Mandarin. The suit dutifully ran to a nearby black SUV, returning with a satellite phone. He handed it to Chen, who pressed a few buttons before handing it to Kryton.

The Australian looked at her curiously as he placed the phone to his ear. A dull dial tone accompanied a few beeps, indicating that a call was transferring through satellites. He took a few steps away from Chen in order to gain some privacy. A voice came across the other end of the line.

"Jonas here."

"Jonas!?" exclaimed Kryton in surprise.

"Mate, you're okay!" said a relieved voice from the SOCCE on Guam.

"Yeah, thanks to my new Chinese friend here. What the hell is going on?"

Jonas could sense Kryton's confusion, if not his dismay. Intelligence operatives hated not having the full picture.

"I understand, we were just told about the back-channel discussions being conducted by the CIA and the MSS. You know what it's like. 'Need-to-know' only."

He knew all too well. He rolled his eyes. He was risking his life for an American endeavour, and they couldn't even be arsed providing what was probably a key piece of information.

He didn't take it personally, though. Knowing that there were adjacent efforts occurring to find intelligence on the situation wouldn't have made any difference when caught up in the middle of a naval gunfire strike.

"Okay. So, what now?" asked Kryton.

"The President is about to be briefed that the intelligence picture has a high degree of confidence that the Chinese government are not behind the attack in Dili."

"Good. What about Wallis? He got away."

"It's obvious someone is trying to play us off against each other. Now that we're both on the same page, I want you to work with the Chinese to work out who else might be involved from their end. And why. Wallis obviously didn't do all this alone."

Kryton looked over at Chen, who was huddled in an intense conversation with her staff members.

"Okay, can do," he said to Jonas.

"We'll have local assets get some better communications kit to you, and we'll update you on the situation as it evolves. Make your next contact to us in twenty-four hours."

"Roger," replied Kryton.

"And Kryton – be careful. This is all starting to look very shady indeed."

*No shit*, thought Kryton to himself as he rubbed his bruised ribs.

"Will do," he said to Jonas as he ended the call.

Chen walked over to him. He handed her the phone, smiling in appreciation.

"I've been assigned to you. What now?" he asked her.

"We've detained someone who I believe you met earlier tonight," she said.

He looked at her, trying not to smile. He couldn't help but be impressed by how informed she was. Then again, he doubted much went on in Taiwan that the Chinese didn't know about. The island was rife with networks keeping Beijing well informed.

"Good. I'd be happy to have a chat with him," Kryton said.

Chen guided him to the back of one of the SUVs. He hopped in first. Protocol usually dictated that the most senior person entered the car last. Chen sat in a position in the rear passenger seat, next to Kryton.

She said something in Mandarin to the driver.

The convoy of three identical cars quickly left the scene and sped off into the streets of Taipei.

# 2

President Jack Lang sat down in his chair in the Oval Office. He adjusted it as he sat forward and upright, placing his glasses over his eyes and focusing on the bound leather folder in front of him.

He tore at the tape which covered the folder. The top of the folder said 'Top Secret' in upper cased red letters. The emblem of the Central Intelligence Agency sat positioned underneath it. CIA Director Anna Dawn sat in the chair next to the Resolute desk, patiently waiting as the President read the bullet points outlining the key notes listed in the Daily Intelligence Brief.

He scanned the document for a few minutes, nodding his head and quietly mumbling to himself as he read over each clearly outlined issue currently occurring globally that required his attention.

"The issue with the American students in South Africa – has it been sorted?" he asked her.

"Yes, sir. The embassy was able to negotiate with the South African foreign office and they won't be prosecuted. They'll simply be deported," she informed him.

"God damn dope heads. The problem with some millennials is they expect someone else to come and rescue them from their fuckups," he said.

"The State Department intends on making life difficult for them on their return. They'll have some explaining to do," she said, smiling at the President's comments.

"Good, good," he said as he closed the folder and softly pushed it across his desk.

He took his glasses off and rubbed his eyes, then ran his hand through his thinning hair. He exhaled deeply. Director Dawn looked at him sympathetically. She could tell he wasn't getting much sleep.

"Sir," she commenced, "I have an update on 'Poseidon'."

He turned his chair slightly and looked at her, gesturing for her to continue.

"We've had success in following up several leads stemming from the JSOC mission onto 'Zulu One'. Our intelligence channels now confirm that the NSA officer involved was one of our best operators, and that he's working with some rogue elements of the PLA."

Director Dawn laid out Wallis's file in front of the President. He quickly glanced over it.

"Shit," he whispered whilst slightly shaking his head in disbelief. "Do we have him in custody?"

"Not yet, sir. Our lead operator engaged with the target in Taipei, but was injured in the contact."

"This is the Australian you have leading the Poseidon mission?" he queried.

"Yes, sir. Zach Kryton. He's okay, and he has now made contact with the Chinese security agents working on this at their end."

"Why is Kryton in Taipei?"

"Kryton followed intelligence that Wallis was headed to Taiwan after escaping the Chinese navy attack on the island. He then engaged Wallis whilst stopping an attack on a diplomatic meeting last night in Taipei. Wallis was working with some Chinese personnel to try to do this."

The President raised his eyebrows.

"Stopped another attack!? This man's proving himself invaluable," said Lang.

Director Dawn nodded in agreement.

"What was the meeting about?"

"We now know that the Chinese and Taiwanese are engaged in some high-level diplomatic talks. Our understanding from our sources is that it's to propose a path to a peaceful resolution of the rising tensions, and perhaps even establish a path to a two-state solution," she informed him.

"What, like with China and Hong Kong?" he asked her.

"Possibly."

Lang leaned back in his chair and shook his head, before stroking his chin in thought.

"I can see plenty of entities that wouldn't support that," he mused. "The hardliners want full re-unification, whilst the independentists in Taiwan will see that as moving backward."

"There would certainly be many against it," she said.

The President tapped his fingers on the wooden edge of his desk.

"So, you now believe that it's not the Chinese behind all this after all?"

She nodded.

"Yes, sir. I do."

"Okay, we need to get this back into a diplomatic discussion. Just *how* confident are we? I don't want to be laying down just as they prepare to run the bus over us," he said.

She paused for a second. No intelligence officer liked to use the word *certain*. He sensed her hesitation.

"Your best assessment, then," he said.

"Highly confident," she responded. "We know there are Chinese elements who supported the attack on us, but not at a state-sanctioned level. They're dealing with traitors, too, it would seem."

He leaned forward and pressed a button on the intercom on his desk.

"Yes, sir?" came the polite voice through the speaker.

"Helen, I need the Chinese President on the phone, immediately," he said.

"It'll need to be secure comms," interrupted Director Dawn in a soft voice.

The President nodded.

"On the secure system, please, Helen. Make it in the Situation Room," he added.

"Yes, sir," replied his secretary.

Lang released the button.

He stood up and walked towards the window, looking out over the cloudy sky.

"Okay, so we have a potential terrorist element consisting of rogue Chinese and American intelligence agents and military personnel trying to attack sovereign government officials," he summarised.

"Yes, sir, that's an accurate assessment."

He turned and looked at her.

"Why are they doing it?"

"Sir, that piece of information we don't know. Kryton is working with the Chinese in Taipei. They have a lead which they're following up."

He walked back over to his seat and sat down. He exhaled deeply.

"Thank goodness it's not the Chinese. We can work with them now."

She nodded. She also felt somewhat relieved. The thought of potential war between two superpowers had kept them both up for the

9

better half of the previous two weeks. A terrorist situation was relatively easy to deal with in comparison.

A knock came from the door on the other side of the room.

"Yes?" said President Lang.

His secretary opened up the door and stood in the doorway.

"The Chinese President is on the secure line, sir. They're waiting for you in the Situation Room."

Lang nodded and smiled. The secretary closed the door behind her.

He stood up from his desk, grabbing the brief in his hands.

He looked at Director Dawn as she stood up too.

"Right. Let's go and get back the initiative."

# 3

The three-car convoy of darkened SUVs drove at speed along the highway on the outskirts of Taipei City. The reflection of the street lights illuminated the roadway, which was relatively quiet due to the late hour.

Kryton looked out of the window as Agent Chen took a call on her phone. He could decipher only a few words of rapidly spoken Mandarin. The tone of her voice suggested that she was speaking to someone of authority. He assumed she was receiving further orders.

Various thoughts ran through his head. He was grateful that the threat of war seemed to have passed by, but it didn't change the fact that there was a highly-skilled, well-motivated, and seemingly well-funded group out trying to provoke a war.

Well-funded because how else could anyone explain them being able to obtain a Chinese Ming class submarine?

Still many questions to be answered, but for now, the focus needed to be on finding out what other imminent threats were out there.

"Beijing has approved my request to undertake advanced questioning of the detainee," said Chen to Kryton as she finished her call.

"Advanced? As in torture?"

She gave him a sly glance.

"You may disapprove of our methods, Mister Kryton, but as you found out after 'Nine-Eleven', they work."

He returned her gaze before looking back out of the window. He adjusted his posture in his seat, trying to hide his discomfort.

"I wouldn't know about that. I'm not an American."

"Yes, I noticed. You're an Australian. Are you a mercenary?"

He looked back at her, trying to ascertain if her body language would tell him just how much she actually knew about him.

11

It seemed to be a genuine question. The Americans had already informed her that he was part of their mission to chase the suspects of the attack. He assumed that they hadn't gone into details about his background, but rather had told her just enough to know that he was an ally – in this instance at least.

"No. I'm former Australian Army."

He said nothing else. Although he didn't believe her to be a threat, his training prevented him from giving too much away. China and the Anglophone nations were not enemies – but they would never be full allies.

"So, what are you now? ASIS? Military Intelligence? Special Forces? It's obvious you have skills, at least enough to be working alone on such a dangerous task that almost got you killed tonight," she said.

"At least, before I saved you," she added softly, a sly grin on her face.

He looked up at her, trying not to smile. She was trying to bait him; to test his ego by making him want to show off to her.

The oldest trick in the book. Getting the person to *want* to talk rather than dragging the information out of them.

He didn't bite. The manner in which she did it suggested to him it was actually a sign of respect – typical banter between two intelligence professionals who were sizing each other up. It also told him that she didn't know any more about who he was.

"Yeah, something like that," he simply said, smiling back at her.

She nodded her head in gracious defeat. She would have to find another way to work out who he was.

"Okay, so I will assume the Australians and the Americans are working together. And now, *we* are working together," she said.

"But?" he replied, sensing more.

"But, in China, we do things the Chinese way. Agreed?"

He looked at her, about to reply, but thought better of it and stopped himself. She was in the position of power, and arguing with her in front of her subordinates wouldn't make for a good working relationship.

Besides, at the end of the day, she had saved his life. For that alone, he respected her, and would respect her position.

"Of course. I'm at your service," he said humbly.

She nodded her head and smiled at him. The driver said something to her in Mandarin as the convoy entered a derelict warehouse area.

"We're here," she said.

# 4

"Thank you, Mister President. This has been most reassuring," said President Lang into the secure phone in the Situation Room.

"Thank you also, Mister President. We'll talk again tomorrow," said the security cleared translator sitting next to him, relaying the words of the Chinese leader.

President Lang hung up the receiver and exhaled deeply. He stood up, stretched his arms out above his head, and yawned. The translator and several aides left the room at the direction of the President.

"Thank goodness for that," he said.

The sense of relief in the room was palpable. Director Dawn allowed herself a small smile. Also sitting informally around the table and having listened to the call were the Chairman of the Joint Chiefs, Admiral Pike; the NSA Director, Jon Blake; as well as Secretary of State, Bradley Kingston.

All were showing signs of fatigue, having spent the past two weeks feverishly trying to ascertain who had attacked Air Force One and trying to stave off a potential conflict with China.

Now that it had been confirmed that China was in fact *not* the enemy, the two large superpowers could now focus their not insignificant intelligence infrastructure towards chasing who was actually behind it.

"Alright," said Lang, looking at Director Blake, "where are we at?"

"NSA tracking indicates that Peter Wallis might have had contact with an entity in Hong Kong, possibly in the period leading up to the attack on Air Force One, as well as after it. We've been tracing affiliations of phones he's been linked with, and tracing those to other phones, and then those phones to others they're connected with, and so on and so forth," he briefed the President.

13

"That sounds complicated," said the President, sitting back down and reclining back in his leather chair at the end of the conference table.

"Yes, sir, but our systems process information pretty fast."

"So, tell me about Hong Kong."

"We're still seeking to ascertain the specifics of who in particular Wallis may have had contact with. We have many leads and are now working through them. Fortunately, we're now in a position to leverage Chinese support," said Director Blake.

The President listened intently, taking in all the information.

He turned to look at Director Dawn.

"Anna, if there are PLA personnel involved, as you suggested previously, will the Chinese be willing to unconditionally help us?"

The CIA Director thought for a second.

"Well, sir, they will be very keen to deal with any internal issues themselves. I'm confident they don't hold us any more responsible for the attempted bombing in Taipei than we do them for the Dili incident. There's both Chinese and Americans involved in whatever this conspiracy is, but both sides know it's not government-sponsored."

"I'm sure they'll not want to lose any more face," observed Admiral Pike.

The CIA Director looked at the Admiral and nodded in agreement.

"Exactly. As we speak, they're looking into their own people who might be involved. Zach Kryton is involved at their end and will be able to keep us informed on anything that generates something that leads to Wallis."

"Good," said Lang. "Anna, ensure he has any support we need."

"Yes, sir."

"Admiral, stand the fleet down a level of readiness. There's no need to maintain this high level of posture. I still want them available in the region, just in case," directed the President to the Chairman.

"Yes, sir."

Lang stood up and walked around the table, deep in thought. He stroked his chin slowly, as was his habit when he was thinking.

"Anna. Your thoughts?"

"Mister President, for now, let's give our Australian colleague and his new Chinese friends some time to follow the leads on their end. We're struggling to find out much about Wallis's movements. He has no family, and the FBI found almost nothing at his residence. But then again, he's skilled in being a ghost. Both digitally and physically."

14

Lang nodded.

"One of the key questions is about who funded it. If we determine that, we might also find out *why* it happened," she added.

"Okay, we just have to let intelligence do what intelligence does."

He said it sincerely. Lang was a pragmatic man and knew that sometimes getting reliable information took time. A lesson learnt in the nearly ten-year chase of Bin Laden.

"Brad, walk with me to the Oval."

Lang left the Situation Room, joined by his Secretary of State. They walked fast, up the steps from the sub-basement level and past the numerous West Wing staff working on a gloomy Friday morning.

"So, why would someone be trying to provoke us and the Chinese?" asked the President.

Kingston shook his head.

"I don't know, but it's obvious they're trying to play us off against each other. I mean, our first instinct was to assume it was the Chinese, and having an NSA agent trying to blow up a high-level diplomatic function would certainly lead them to blame us."

The two men walked past several offices, with the Secret Service agents keeping close by.

"We've been lucky, Brad. One Australian soldier who happens to be in the right place at the right time, not once but twice. Talk about fortunate," mused the President.

"Yeah, lucky. But why? What's their reason for doing it?"

"I don't know, Brad, but that traitor is still out there, and I want his arse in a sling."

The two men walked into the reception area of the Oval Office. The President's secretary stood up to greet him.

"The Vice President is waiting for you, sir," she informed him.

The President stopped. A confused look appeared on his face as he looked at his watch.

"Shit, it's that time already," he mumbled.

He turned to face Secretary Kingston.

"Okay, Brad. We'll have that drink this afternoon. For now, I need you to inform our five-eye partners about the current intelligence assessment. Specifically brief the Australians; after all, it's their man essentially leading all this."

"Yes, Mister President."

The two old friends shook hands before Kingston walked off to make his way back to the State Department.

The President thanked his secretary before walking into the Oval Office.

"Matthew, thanks for coming in," he said as he walked over to the Resolute desk where Vice President Matthew Kendrick was standing.

"Not a problem, Mister President," replied Kendrick.

About the same age, but of smaller stature than the President, Kendrick had been persuaded by Lang and the Republican Party to leave the private sector to be Lang's running mate, not least of all due to his distinguished years of military service, the final years which had been spent as the Director of the NSA.

President Lang sat down and took a sip from the glass of water that had been laid out for him. He gestured for Kendrick to sit in the seat next to the desk.

"So, we've confirmed that it wasn't the Chinese who organised the attack," Lang briefed Kendrick.

"What? Are we sure?"

"We are. I've just spoken to the Chinese President. We're now on the same page."

The Vice President appeared confused, but also relieved.

"So, who was it?"

Lang leaned back in his chair and crossed his legs.

"Well, it seems there's a joint effort between traitors on both sides. The Chinese are also chasing former PLA and intelligence types who colluded with a former NSA agent named Wallis."

The Vice President had been completely briefed into the ongoing situation. The failed assassination attempt had reinforced for the administration the need to have a second-in-command who could take over from POTUS if, God forbid, it was required.

Kendrick sat back in his seat. He ran his fingers over his mouth, taking in the new bit of information.

"Well, that is certainly a relief, sir."

There was a knock at the door.

"Yes?"

The President's secretary walked in and handed Lang a manila folder.

"Thank you, Helen," he said politely.

She respectfully excused herself and walked back out of the room.

"Now, Matthew. I'll be sending you to New York on Tuesday to brief the U.N. on the developing issue. The Security Council will sit, and with the Chinese and ourselves putting forward a united front that everything that has occurred has been a concerted terrorist effort, we can help soothe the concerns of all our international partners. We can get the markets back on track and the region can breathe a well-needed sigh of relief."

The Vice President opened the folder that the President's secretary had brought in and looked over the talking points that had been arranged by the State Department.

"Yes, sir. Sounds fair. I'll speak privately with the Chinese ambassador to gauge their opinion on the way forward."

"Yes, please do so. I'll be preparing for the state visit of the Australian Prime Minister next week."

Lang stood up, followed by Kendrick. They slowly walked to the door.

"I'm also interested to see what you can learn about their interactions with the Taiwanese. It seems they've been in deep discussions, but we don't know exactly what about."

Kendrick looked at Lang.

"Are we thinking that it's about them repairing their relations?"

"Maybe, we're trying to find that out now," said Lang.

"Well, that can only be a good thing."

"We'll see. It could have been very different if Wallis had bombed their secret meeting last night."

"Wallis?" asked Kendrick, seemingly surprised.

"Yep. He was the one trying to bomb the meeting in Taipei last night, but was stopped by the Australian operative before any significant damage could be done."

"So, Wallis…he's still alive?"

"I'm afraid so. We're pursuing several lines of enquiry now in Taiwan."

Kendrick stopped walking and looked at the President. Lang sensed that the Vice President was unhappy.

"It's okay, Matt. We'll get the bastard. We haven't chased an individual this hard since Bin Laden."

Kendrick exhaled deeply and gave the President a small smile.

"Yes, sir. I'm sure we will."

The Vice President shook hands with Lang as the two parted ways at the entrance to the Oval Office. He walked past the President's secretary, giving her a small nod as he walked into the hallway of the West Wing. His security detail joined him.

He pulled a phone from his coat pocket and dialled his own secretary.

"Cecilia. I need you to clear my schedule for the next few days and make preparations for a trip," he said into his phone.

He took several more steps down the busy corridor, the phone still pressed to his ear. West Wing staffers politely acknowledged him as they walked past. He continued his conversation.

"Where?... We're going to New York."

# 5

Several darkened SUVs were parked neatly near the entrance of a derelict factory on the outskirts of Taipei. Two neatly dressed Chinese men stood guard, silently observing the stars whilst standing in the mild night air.

A dog barked in the distance, echoing through the otherwise abandoned industrial neighbourhood not far from the northern part of the Taiwan Strait.

A dim glow emanated from a small room inside. Two figures stood in the dusty kitchenette of the former fish factory, quietly observing a small CCTV box hastily positioned on a table in the corner.

Kryton and Chen watched as two large Chinese agents took turns slapping around a helpless man tied to a chair in the middle of the main factory floor. Dressed in a now torn restaurant waiter's uniform, the man whimpered as another blow rained down from above and across his face.

*That one would have hurt*, Kryton thought to himself as he watched the interrogation unfolding in front of him on the small box television.

Kryton felt no sympathy for the man, nor did he feel any malice.

This was purely business.

"I bet you're wondering when the fingernail pulling starts," said Chen to him in a very dry manner.

He looked at her, allowing himself a sly grin, amused by her humour.

"I heard you don't go in for that thing anymore," he replied.

She smiled as she looked back down at the screen.

Kryton knew he was only a guest in this. He wouldn't do or say anything unless it crossed any major ethical or legal boundaries. He was still bound by his own national legal restrictions, which were significantly more restrictive than the Chinese and U.S. ones.

However, this meant he had become adept at learning how to push the boundaries. He would allow Chen to do what she needed to do, and he would simply observe from the background.

Chen said something in Mandarin into a two-way radio. The two agents inside the main floor looked up, nodded, and quickly left the tied up man alone.

"Okay, Mister Kryton, are you ready to see what we can find?"

Kryton nodded.

He was curious to see how she would handle the interrogation. Chinese culture typically put men in the main positions of authority, so he assumed that seeing a woman asking him questions would unbalance the waiter, possibly putting him off guard and making it easier to get him to answer questions.

It was a trick that had been used with great success in Afghanistan, where pretty young female interrogators had conducted questioning sessions against Taliban members. The sight of a young female in an authoritative position, often deliberately wearing a strong feminine fragrance, made even some of the hardest Taliban sing like canaries.

The two burly agents walked into the kitchenette. Chen had a quick conversation with them. Their hands weren't swollen, though, and it was obvious the blood covering them wasn't theirs. It suggested they had actually gone lightly on the waiter.

Kryton assumed that Chen had instructed them to pull their punches. The fact that the waiter already had a bruised face and a broken nose, courtesy of the back-street fight with Kryton, meant that any blow to the face would have hurt like hell regardless of how soft it was.

The two intelligence agents left the small kitchenette, walked up a hallway, and approached a door being guarded by another one of the large Chinese men.

Chen nodded at him, and the man opened the door to let them in.

Kryton glanced at the large Chinese agent as he passed by him whilst walking into the main part of the factory. The man didn't even flinch.

*Serious buggers*, Kryton thought to himself, quietly thinking the man's strict outward expression was probably an equal dose of professionalism as well as the expected demeanour of a loyal subject of the Chinese Communist Party.

The Australian followed Chen onto the main factory floor. It smelt like the inside of a tuna can. The humid early morning air wafted over Kryton's face, forcing him to cover his mouth as his nostrils adjusted to the putrid air. He followed Chen to the side of the factory, where the young Chinese man was slumped in a chair.

The sound of drops of rain falling from the cracks in the roof many feet above their heads echoed throughout the mostly empty factory. Other than the ambient noise of the water dripping onto the concrete floor and the abandoned machinery, the large open space was silent. A dull glow emanated from the flickering fluorescent globe that was on the nearby wall, providing just enough light to allow them to look at the hapless figure.

Chen walked up to him and grabbed his chin, lifting it to expose his face. He looked back at her, breathing heavily. Blood trickled down his face from his nose, staining his white shirt. The man looked less scared than he did exhausted. The two agents had slapped him around enough to give him a decent headache.

Chen reached down behind the man's chair and picked up a strategically placed bottle of water. She said something softly in Mandarin, placing the bottle to the man's lips.

He took several small sips between heavy breaths.

She placed the bottle back down and stood back, looking down at the man. Kryton stood a few paces behind her. The man shook his head swiftly and looked back up at her. He looked confused.

The change in the pace of the interrogation had caught him off guard – just as she had planned.

*Good work*, Kryton thought to himself.

Chen whispered something else to the man, who then looked up at the strange white man standing nearby.

The prisoner adjusted his eyes, trying to focus on Kryton. A look of recognition appeared on his face. He looked back at Chen, even more confused.

She said something again to him, the inflection making it sound like she was asking him a question.

"Yes, I speak some," he feebly replied in English in a heavy accent.

"Good, then we can talk in English for the benefit of my friend here," she said whilst gesturing to Kryton.

The man looked back up at Kryton, still breathing heavily. He inhaled deeply, trying to compose himself.

"Who are you? What do you want?" he asked.

He seemed to have composed himself, which suggested to Kryton that he had had some professional training in resisting interrogation. Like

21

Kryton had done with the Iranian back at the Black Site in the middle of the Pacific, the aim would be to make the man open up in reward for small comforts, such as not being smacked around by two burly Chinese agents.

"Your mission failed," Chen said bluntly. "The bomb didn't explode. Your efforts to stall the reunification did not work."

Kryton quickly assessed what her approach was. It was obvious that she was trying to convince him that there was no reason for him to not talk because there was no operational information left to protect.

As an interrogation methodology, it is known as the soft and logical approach.

The man looked at Kryton, trying to ascertain any cue from the Australian that might confirm or discredit Chen's statement.

Kryton stared straight back at him, pan faced.

Chen moved around behind the man, softly placing her hand on his shoulder.

"Why were you trying to attack the delegation?" she asked him.

The man sat in silence. Chen moved around to the front of the chair and looked down at him. He still said nothing. Kryton placed his hands in his pockets, curious as to what she might do next.

He didn't have to wait long to find out.

With the speed of an angry snake, Chen raised her arm across her body, cracking it down across the man's nose with a backhand strike.

He cried out in pain as fresh blood poured from his nose.

Chen stood back, looking down at him. She picked up the bottle of water, splashing some of the warm liquid across his face.

She paused for a moment as the man again swiftly shook his head. The strike was fairly hard and would have rattled his brain. He started to breathe heavily again.

"If you talk to me, this will not happen, and we can get you medical attention," she said to him.

She kneeled on her haunches, looking at him, almost sympathetically. She whispered something at him in Mandarin. This made the man look up at Kryton, a glint of fear in his eyes. The Australian tensed his fists and glared straight back at the man.

Although he didn't speak enough Mandarin to hear clearly what she had said to him, he'd conducted enough interrogations to know that his reaction to her soft words meant she had probably said something along the lines of: 'I'm here to help, but if you don't talk, I'll let this white guy beat the shit out of you.'

She stood up, looking back down at him. The man looked down at his feet, weighing up his options. He glanced back up at Kryton.

He'd had enough for one night.

"Okay," he said sheepishly.

"Good," she said calmly, now speaking English again.

"Where are you from?"

"Ghuangzhou," he said.

"Who sent you?"

The man exhaled deeply, again reluctant to speak. He looked up at her.

"Please, I was only following orders," he said.

"Why were you trying to attack the delegation?"

He looked at her in confusion.

"What delegation? We were conducting a special operation for China," he attempted to explain to her.

"Liar," she screamed at him, quickly changing the pace of the questioning once again.

Kryton took a pace forward to help reinforce her action. This caused the man to quickly shift in his seat, anticipating another beating.

"No...No, I'm not," he protested loudly.

"Then who sent you?" she asked him firmly. "Why were you trying to attack our delegation? Why are you a traitor?"

The man again shifted in his seat, looking rapidly between Chen and Kryton.

"What? No, I'm...what?"

He appeared very confused, even in response to some of her simpler questions. Kryton thought for a moment. He remembered his interrogation of the Iranian. Remembered how uninformed the Persian man had turned out to be.

He cleared his throat, attempting to grab her attention. She looked up at him. He motioned with his head for her to come and join him. They took a few paces, out of the light and out of earshot of the man.

Kryton whispered into Chen's ear.

"I think he believes that you're Taiwanese," he said softly.

She turned her head to glance at the Australian. Thoughts raced through her own head. She looked down at the ground before looking back at Kryton. Without saying a word, she walked back over to the man.

23

Kryton followed.

She leaned down and again spoke softly to him.

"Who do you think I work for?" she asked.

He looked at her as if it was a silly question.

"You're…you're Taipei police."

Her eyes darted towards Kryton. His theory was correct. Chen exhaled deeply as she stood up.

"We're *Daluren*," she said to him, referring to the Mandarin word meaning someone from the Chinese mainland.

The man tried to say something, but the dryness in his mouth made the words inaudible.

"I…I don't believe you," he said.

Chen reached into her coat pocket and took out a small wallet, opening it up and displaying her diplomatic identification. The look on his face was a mix of confusion and relief.

Chen stood up and walked with Kryton quickly back to the door leading out of the factory floor. They moved past the guarding agents and back into the kitchenette.

She turned to face Kryton.

"Who *is* he?" he asked her.

"Whoever he is, he thought we were the local police. He seemed almost relieved when I told him I was Chinese government."

Kryton looked down at the small monitor and the man again sitting alone on the factory floor.

"If he was relieved to see a Chinese government official, then who does he think he's working for?" he asked her.

"I don't know. We sent his image to Beijing; they should be able to provide us some information soon."

"Did he have any other information on him?" he asked.

Chen spoke loudly in Mandarin to the agent outside. He entered the room and she had a short conversation with him. He nodded his head subserviently and walked out.

"He says they searched him thoroughly, but he didn't have anything else on him, apart from the identification card and the phone you used to find your way to the 101 building."

"Will you be able to do an interrogation of the phone and find any links or connections?"

"Yes. We can share that with the Americans, too. They might be able to match that to an intelligence picture."

"Okay. My concern is the American you saved me from back in Taipei. He's the main threat."

"Why would an American try to kill his own President?" Chen asked Kryton.

He just shrugged his shoulders and shook his head.

"Who knows? They have a history of knocking off their leaders every few decades."

She looked at him, confused by his Western terminology. He noticed her confusion.

"To assassinate them," he clarified for her.

"Oh," she said. "Do you know who this American assassin is?"

He looked at her for a moment, wondering whether he should tell her. Since it was now a combined operation, he figured it wouldn't matter.

"His name is Peter Wallis. He's a former NSA agent who somehow and for some reason has gone rogue. We believe he's responsible for the sabotage on Air Force One."

Chen observed silently, her eyes widened. It was obvious Beijing was not yet aware of this information – or at least she wasn't.

"He was also on the island your navy shelled whilst my team was on it," he added.

Chen listened intently, taking in all the information he was sharing with her.

"We detained an Iranian man in Dili who was hired by Wallis to conduct the attack. That man was supported by several Chinese men, who we also detained in Dili. We know they are PLA of some sort. If they had access to one of your submarines, they must have been getting help from some senior officials."

Chen sat down at the table.

"About three months ago, one of our *Ming* class submarines was stolen from its base at the South Sea Fleet headquarters in Zhanjiang. Several guards on the wharf were found murdered."

Kryton sat down next to her.

"How? Did you tell the Americans?"

She tried to conceal a small laugh.

"Do you think they would announce to the world if they had a *Virginia* class submarine go missing?" she asked rhetorically.

Kryton leaned back in the seat.

"No, I suppose not."

"Beijing assumed it was the Triads, or perhaps even a rogue element of the PLA looking to use it to sell to drug runners. It's only the events of the past few weeks that have made us realise that it has been used for something more sinister," she said.

Kryton rubbed his jaw.

"And you said before that you didn't know about the island where the sub was hiding until you received a tip-off?"

"That's correct," she said. "Someone on the inside must have known and decided to betray them," she said, mirroring the theory Kryton had considered in the SUV earlier.

Kryton looked again at the monitor.

"So, what now?"

"One of my subordinates will be here soon with an update based on this man's photograph and fingerprints. We'll know who he is then."

Chen stood up.

"I'm going to allow one of my juniors to continue the questioning."

She rubbed her nose, as if trying to remove the foul odour that was stuck inside her nostrils.

"Until then, I suggest we go and get some fresh air."

# 6

Kryton stood in the humid morning air out the front of the factory. He observed the hills to the west and watched as the first dull glow of civil twilight crept above the ridgeline.

He rubbed his eyes as he yawned. It had been a long night. He carefully touched his face and his ribs. They were still sore. It simply motivated him to continue the chase for Wallis.

A few moments later, Agent Chen joined him.

"How is it going in there?" he asked her.

It had been half an hour since she had sent her subordinates in to talk further to the man dressed as the waiter.

Chen also tried to stifle a yawn.

"His name is Wang Xiu Ying. He says that he's a soldier with the PLA and that he's part of a covert operation to disrupt Taiwanese separatists."

"Do you believe him?" asked Kryton.

"We'll find out soon enough. The details from PLA headquarters will either confirm or deny his story."

"You don't seem convinced, though," he probed.

She thought for a moment.

"I've been in charge of this station for twelve months. Nothing happens here without my knowledge."

He looked at her body language. She seemed frustrated.

"Always? Did you know about the meeting at the 101 last night?" he asked.

Chen kicked at the non-existent dirt at her feet. She looked at him. Now it was her turn to share information.

"We have been secretly talking to the Taiwanese leaders for the last six months in order to set a path to improved relations. This will facilitate better trade and help improve the overall relationship."

"As a path to reunification?" he asked, knowing full well that it was CCP policy to one day have reunification with the small ethnically Chinese island off of the Chinese mainland.

"No one wants a war in the region, Mister Kryton," she stated firmly.

He respected her for towing the party line. He decided not to push the issue. It wasn't relevant at the moment, anyway.

"What else did he say?" he asked.

"He states that he was taking orders from his command and that his team was ordered to disrupt a meeting between separatists. He says he only arrived in Taipei yesterday."

"Who else is he working with?"

"He gave us two names. It seems that they were there to facilitate the materials that he had on him that you found."

Kryton looked up at the sky. The morning star was shining brightly as the horizon slowly turned a deep shade of purple.

"That doesn't make sense. Would a disruption mean exploding a bomb? Surely they would have known about your government officials having been there. I took his identification card off of him, so that means he was supposed to be inside the function room."

Chen shrugged her shoulders.

"I agree, it doesn't make sense."

She looked at Kryton.

"The man you interrogated from Dili – the Iranian – did he know much?"

He knew why she was asking.

"No. He was only briefed into his specific part. In fact, he thought he was shooting down a cargo plane. I'm guessing these guys were told lies, too. Where are his companions now?"

"We don't know," said Chen. "Their standard operating procedure would be to abandon the operation and seek to meet up with their compatriots to enact the exfiltration plan."

"So, there could be some of your soldiers running around Taipei looking to get off of the island?" he stated.

Chen nodded.

"Possibly. It doesn't matter. We have their names from our questioning of the suspect. We'll soon know who they are specifically and perhaps even what their intent is."

A pair of headlights appeared up the road away from the factory. They slowly approached where Kryton and Chen were standing. One of the agents spoke into his radio, before raising his hand and guiding the car into the gated factory.

It was another SUV.

It pulled up next to where Kryton and Chen were standing. All four doors opened simultaneously, and four well-dressed figures disembarked.

Two men. Two women.

Chen approached one of the men, who was carrying a briefcase. He acknowledged Chen very respectfully. Obviously he was her subordinate. The two had a quick conversation in Mandarin.

Chen pointed towards the door, then looked at Kryton and gestured for him to follow her.

"This is my operations officer, Agent Li," she said as the three of them walked towards the front door of the factory.

"I'm Kryton, nice to meet you, mate," said the larger Australian to the diminutive MSS officer as he shook the Chinese man's hand.

The intensity of the grip caught the agent by surprise, but the smile from the Australian reassured him that he meant no harm.

The three walked inside and into the kitchenette.

Chen said a few words in Mandarin, which her subordinate dutifully nodded in response to.

She changed to speaking in English.

"Agent Li has information from Beijing. We have authority to share this with you with a view it will be relayed to your own authorities."

"I understand," he said as they all sat down.

Li opened the securely locked briefcase and pulled out a red A4 folder. He placed it down on the table and pulled out the contents.

He commenced his brief.

"Beijing is now aware of a small element of special forces operators from the Guangzhou Military Region who have been missing for the past few weeks."

"They are known as the 'South China Sword' – a very capable unit," interjected Agent Chen.

Kryton nodded.

Li produced several pictures.

"This is Wang Xiu Ying, a weapons specialist. He's the man we have with us inside answering our questions," he briefed very articulately and in exceptionally good English.

He shuffled the pictures and placed another image on the top. Kryton recognised the man in it instantly.

*The Boss*, he thought to himself – the man he had fought in Dili who had led the operation to attack Air Force One.

"This is Captain Wang Lei. He's an experienced officer who usually trains new members to the unit."

Kryton pulled the image across the table to look at it more closely.

"We know this guy and some of his friends. We detained him in Dili," he said to the two Chinese agents.

Li looked at Chen, almost enthusiastically. It seemed that Kryton had just confirmed an assumption that they had made about the whereabouts of the special forces officer.

"We also checked the details of the other people Ying said were supporting him. They are also part of the same military unit," said Li.

"I think that Lei is probably one of the leaders of this. If he trained new members, he'd be in a good position to select those either willing or naïve enough to take part."

Chen looked at Li. She nodded in agreement with Kryton's assessment.

Li proceeded to produce a few other notes, all written in Mandarin.

"Our communications tracking indicates that the phone that Ying used has links to a tower within Hong Kong, near the Sha Tin district. We've traced the other numbers found on it. Most of those are based in Guangzhou."

Kryton and Chen looked over some of the maps. The word *Google* was neatly placed in the bottom right-hand corner.

*Looks like they use the same mapping service we do*, thought Kryton to himself as he tried to conceal a laugh.

Hastily constructed intelligence briefs often relied on whatever sources of information and supporting technology was currently available – the foremost usually being the internet.

"Anything else that can give us a lead?" asked Kryton hopefully.

"Yes, we have been able to link one of the numbers to the same tower. This number was from a phone linked to Captain Lei. Both of Ying and Lei's numbers are linked to a third number."

"So, two numbers directly linked to each other are also directly linked to a third number?" observed Kryton.

"Yes," replied Li.

"Okay, but why is that the lead we need to follow?" asked Kryton.

Chen finished looking over the materials.

"Because, that third number based in Hong Kong has also had communication with a satellite phone that has been using *this* tower," she said, placing a picture of a familiar phone tower in front of Kryton.

"Wallis?" he said softly as he looked at the picture, clearly showing the tower that he had helped his CIA counterpart hack into on Zulu One.

He looked at the two of them and smiled. He was impressed with their level of telecommunications tracking capability, even though the recent advancements in Chinese signals intelligence were well known amongst the five-eyes community.

"So, Mister Kryton, we now have a common connection between all of the PLA soldiers we have detained in Dili and Taipei – and it's in Hong Kong."

Kryton nodded.

"So, when do we leave?" he said eagerly, almost with a second wind of energy and motivation.

Chen asked Li a question in Mandarin. It was obvious they were already planning for the next step. They engaged in a short conversation.

"Beijing is sending a plane for us. It will be here later tonight."

"Good. I'll need to talk to my people. Can you take me back to my hotel?" he asked her.

Chen called out over his shoulder to one of the agents outside.

"What about Wallis?" he asked her.

"We have all our sources looking for him, as well as the others involved. It will be hard for them to get off the island."

Kryton nodded.

One of the Chinese agents came through the door, quickly saying something to Agent Chen. She stood up and walked Kryton out to one of the waiting SUVs.

The first orange glow of the rising sun appeared across the hills in the distance. It looked like it would be a clear day.

"We will collect you from the hotel at seven this evening. Speak to your authorities, and we'll plan our actions from the plane."

"Thank you, Agent Chen. I appreciate everything," he said as he stepped into the SUV.

Forty-five minutes later, Kryton walked into the foyer of the Grand Hyatt Hotel. He walked up to the concierge desk, catching the overnight desk clerk watching a baseball game being broadcast by satellite from the U.S.

"Any messages for me? Room fourteen twelve."

The clerk fumbled around in a desk drawer, pulling out a padded envelope. It was simply marked with his room number.

"Thank you. Would you mind sending some ice up to my room, please?" he said to the clerk before making his way to the elevator.

Once inside, he ripped open the top of the envelope and pulled out a small micro SD card.

He knew it would contain encrypted data that would be the daily changeable codes that would allow him to again communicate to the SOCCE.

Kryton walked through the elevator doors and towards his room. He quickly located the strand of hair he had placed across the top of the doorframe – a clear sign that no-one had been in his room. He unlocked the door using his key card and entered.

He walked across to the window sill and looked out at the morning sky. He took his jacket off, placed his pistol down next to it on the table, and inhaled deeply, thinking of the events of the past twelve hours.

His thoughts were interrupted by a knock on the door. Kryton went over, opened it, and took the ice from the young housekeeper. He nodded in thanks before shutting the door.

He placed the ice down on the table, went to the bathroom, and grabbed a small hand towel. He sat down by the table, placed some of the ice into the towel, folded it up to form an improvised ice pack, and gingerly placing it against the exposed skin next to his ribs.

He tipped the small bottle of Jack Daniels whiskey from the minibar into a glass, added some of the ice, and sat back, nursing his injuries.

Kryton spent the next fifteen minutes entering the codes into his tablet, connecting a secure link to the SOCCE. He sent an updated situation report. After five minutes, the SOCCE replied and told him that the next communication would occur later that afternoon.

The exhausted operator leaned back on the bed, thinking about everything that had happened over the previous few weeks. He was still sore, but he had no injuries that would have any long-term impact.

*Might try and get some rest*, he thought to himself.

He was virtually asleep before his head hit the pillow.

# 7

The shrill sound of a beeping electronic device stirred Kryton from his slumber. His body shot upright, reaching madly for his pistol. He grasped it and pointed it at the table where his tablet was beeping. It took him a few moments to remember where he was. He became fully aware of his surroundings, remembering that he was in a hotel room. He laid back down.

He rolled over to look at the clock radio on the bedside table. The bright red numbers told him that it was just after four in the afternoon.

He laughed, before running his hand through his hair.

Kryton jumped up from the bed and retrieved the tablet from the table. He pressed the appropriate button and watched as the image of Jonas appeared on the screen.

"Jesus – you look like hell," observed Jonas.

Kryton furrowed his brow in confusion, before catching a glimpse of himself in the smaller screen in the corner of the chat window. A few bruises were starting to appear on his face from where he had been knocked over in his fight with Wallis.

"Oh. Don't worry about that. It couldn't have got any worse anyway," he said while brushing his hand over his face.

His humour was still intact, if not his face.

"Are you still in this? Are you still good to go?" asked Jonas.

"Absolutely. I've managed to get some rest. I'm good to go."

"Okay, good. So, where are we at?" asked Jonas.

"I'll be going to Hong Kong with the Chinese girl. We've managed to find a lead based on the guy that led me to the covert diplomatic meeting, and he's linked to those Chinese blokes from Dili, too."

Jonas ruffled through some of the papers he had on the desk in front of him.

33

"The Chinese have sent us a portfolio on their current understanding of the situation. Likewise, we've shared our intelligence with them. What's your read on their point of view of all of this?"

Kryton sat down on the edge of the bed and thought for a moment.

"I don't believe they were responsible for the attack. In fact, it seems like they've been caught as unaware by all of this as we have. You know what the Chinese are like, they'll try to save face by blaming someone else, or by hiding their shortcomings."

Jonas nodded in agreement. Kryton looked at some of the handwritten notes he had scribbled down earlier during the ride back to the hotel.

"It seems that a small group of PLA soldiers have possibly gone rogue, conducting their own operations that are not being endorsed by Beijing. The connection to the tower at Zulu One indicates they are working with Wallis. I think that they're being funded by someone. This is the lead I'm going to Hong Kong to follow up."

"Jee-sus," said Jonas slowly under his breath. "It must be well funded. They had access to a submarine and some pretty solid technical gear. This doesn't sound like a small group of terrorists."

"I agree," replied Kryton. "However, I think we now have the initiative."

"How so?" asked Jonas.

Kryton took a sip of water from the bottle provided in the room by the hotel concierge services.

"Their tactical mission was to shoot down Air Force One. We don't know the strategic reasons, but we can keep working on that. Ever since they failed to shoot the plane down, everything that we've been able to discover suggests that they expected success. They haven't covered their tracks that well."

Jonas looked at Kryton through the screen closely. He'd always trusted his friend's assessments of any given situation.

"The information from the detainees, along with the communications tracking of Wallis's phone. None of it was ever supposed to have been discovered. I think they're on the run now."

Jonas smiled.

"Okay. What do you need from my end?" he said to Kryton.

He thought for a second.

"Continue chasing the financial details of the Iranian's bank accounts. He told me that he was paid by Wallis. If someone was funding Wallis, we should be able to link any transactions back to the source."

"AUSTRAC is looking at those as we speak," said Jonas, referring to the Australian Transaction and Analysis Centre – the Australian government's financial intelligence service.

"Good. The low-level operators link to Wallis. The links we can find upwards from Wallis will lead us to the head of the snake."

"Or snakes," suggested Jonas.

Kryton nodded in agreement.

"Let's hope not."

"Well," continued Jonas, "whoever it is, we need to find them fast. We foiled two attacks so far. We might not be so lucky a third time."

"Oh…one more thing," said Kryton. "Agent Chen told me that their navy attacked Zulu One based on a tip-off. They had no idea that Wallis or any of his crew were on there."

Jonas's eyes widened.

"You're kidding me. Well that can only mean –"

"That they have a leak themselves," interjected Kryton.

Jonas exhaled deeply as he rubbed his eyes. He, too, was feeling the rigours of long hours chasing ghosts.

"Well, that can only work in our favour in the long run," he said.

"Agreed," replied Kryton.

"Okay, we'll keep seeing what we can find. Once you find anything from your new Chinese friends, you'll have to let us know. Like you said, if they're trying to save face, they might not be sharing everything with us – especially if these links lead to someone or someones too close to home for their comfort."

"Roger. Next comms in twenty-four hours," said Kryton.

Jonas paused for a moment.

"Do you think you can trust them enough to help us?" he asked Kryton.

"If they were PLA, then I'd be very wary. But she's MSS. They're handpicked and very loyal to the party. Any other time, no way in hell. But, we're both now after the same thing."

"Yeah got it. 'The enemy of my enemy is my friend', as they say," replied Jonas.

Kryton smiled.

"Okay, we have no choice for now. Zach…be careful. I've attached a small file, have a quick read of it."

Kryton gave the thumbs up before ending the communication.

He gently placed the tablet back down on the table, before standing up and walking to the window. The sun was beginning its descent in the western sky. Soon, young and old alike would arrive in the city for a leisurely Saturday night in the capital.

Kryton looked at the television. The sound was muted, but the evening news displayed scenes of fire engines and law enforcement officers attending the 101 building the night before. The headlines read: 'fire alarm causes chaos during a politician's birthday event.'

*The Beijing propaganda machine at work*, Kryton thought to himself, smiling, and impressed that the Chinese had been able to conceal the true nature of the events that had actually occurred the night before.

He walked to the bathroom and took off his shirt, looking in the large mirror on the wall.

He observed the man looking back at him.

He almost didn't recognise himself. His ribs were starting to bruise, turning a light shade of purple. He still had some dry blood on his face, sticking to the stubble of his three-day growth. He looked at his nose.

Still slightly crooked.

Wallis hadn't caused that. Years of playing football and training in martial arts had caused that.

He allowed himself a small laugh as he splashed water over his face, washing the dirt, blood, and goodness knows what else off of it.

He stripped completely and stepped into the shower.

The warm flowing water welcomely washed over his body.

He thought long and hard about everything that had happened since Jonas had appeared out of the blue at the Royal Military College at Duntroon a few weeks earlier.

He'd spent a long time waiting for another opportunity to get back into the game. But now, whilst looking at himself in the mirror that was starting to cloud from the steam of the hot shower, he was wondering if it was worth it.

A career in the shadows had left him with many scars – physical and mental.

He washed his body with soap, ignoring the stinging it brought to the small cuts all over his body.

He was just glad to have had a moment to collect his thoughts. To assess where things now sat and try to decide what the next move should be. That last part wasn't in his hands. He had a plane to catch.

Kryton spat some of the shower water out of his mouth. He watched as it circled the drain before gravity took over. The red colouring indicated that the blows from Wallis and the Chinese soldier dressed as a waiter would probably leave some marks on him for a while.

He tried to put himself in his adversary's shoes – as intelligence operators are trained to do.

*Who was Wallis?*

*Why would he betray his country?*

But more importantly,

*What was his next move?*

Kryton finished up his shower. He walked back into the room, hearing a knock on the door. The housekeeper presented him with his clothes – freshly cleaned and pressed.

Twenty minutes later, he was standing outside of the hotel entrance. A black SUV soon pulled up.

It was Agent Chen.

Kryton jumped in. He felt rested and refreshed. He was rejuvenated and ready for the next part of the operation.

"Did you get some sleep?" asked Chen, who looked equally refreshed. She now wore her hair up in a bun, but otherwise, her outfit seemed to be the same.

"Yes. Thank you," replied Kryton.

She smiled at him, before looking back out of the window as the driver pulled out into the evening traffic.

Less than an hour later, they pulled up to the VIP section of the international airport. An unmarked corporate jet awaited them. The two pilots and a female flight attendant stood by the boarding ladder. They greeted Chen respectfully as she allowed Kryton to board the plane first.

He noticed that he was being stared at by the three crew who cautiously gazed over the unknown white man. He took a seat, and a moment later she sat down opposite him. They would be the only two passengers on board for the flight.

The flight attendant wasted no time in closing the door, before giving a quick brief to Chen.

"We should be there in under two hours," she then informed Kryton.

He nodded, placing his seatbelt over his lap and looking out of the window. Dark clouds were quickly replacing the setting sun, indicating that a storm was fast approaching.

The flight attendant presented him a tray. It contained a glass of soda water with ice. Kryton took it.

"Xie Xie," he said, thanking her with his limited Mandarin.

The flight attendant smiled, before moving up the plane and behind a curtain, taking her seat in preparation for take-off.

Less than five minutes later, they were in the air and headed for Hong Kong.

# 8

*Taiwan Straits*
*22°55'56" N, 116°43'37" E*
2105 local

Kryton gazed out the window as the jet made its way towards Hong Kong at an altitude of 35,000 feet. The internal cabin lights had been dimmed, allowing him to see a faint orange glow that hugged the horizon – the last remnants of sunlight which were rapidly disappearing.

The clouds this far away from Taiwan had cleared up, and Kryton could see the first of what would be many stars begin to litter the evening sky.

The plane flew just off of the coastline, but close enough that Kryton could occasionally see a small cluster of lights from a coastal village. He couldn't remember ever having flown in such luxury. It was certainly a far cry from conducting static line and freefall drops behind enemy lines.

He subconsciously rubbed his nose and his jaw.

"Does it still hurt?"

His eyes darted towards the seat opposite him. He saw Agent Chen looking back at him, somewhat sympathetically.

He had thought she was asleep.

"Umm, nah, I'll be fine," he replied, lying to her in order to not appear weak.

The truth was, his whole body still ached. He had learned to live with aches and pains. 'Mind over matter' – or whatever it was his old platoon sergeant had once told him during a particularly gruelling special operations training exercise in the middle of a cold night.

He sat up and adjusted his eyes.

She was looking over her notes. He had observed her as coming across as the consummate professional. Saying nothing unless something needed to be said.

He respected that.

He was curious to learn more, however.

"So, how long have you been on station?" he asked her.

She looked up from her notes. He returned her gaze, waiting curiously for a response.

Two intelligence professionals at work. Always seeking to gain information whilst protecting their own. A sly grin appeared on her face as she closed her folder. She would happily engage in conversation with him.

"A little over two years," she said.

"Two years! I bet you've been kept busy during that time," he said cheekily.

"Oh yes, it has been busy. Always some Western warship arrogantly conducting a freedom-of-navigation exercise near our waters," she said.

He looked at her curiously, observing the sarcastic expression on her face. He tried to conceal a small smile.

*What do you know! A sense of humour*, he thought to himself.

"Well, I can't help you there, you'll have to speak to the Americans about that. We're lucky to get our navy ships to sea at all half the time," he said to her drolly.

She let out a small laugh.

He took a sip of water from the glass on the armrest next to him.

"So, what's next for you after Taipei?"

"I'm sure Beijing has a position for me where I can best serve my country," she said simply.

He smiled and nodded.

The fact was, he already knew all the information.

Her name, her education, her previous postings. Jonas had provided a full dossier back over encrypted means back at the hotel.

With anyone else, or at another time, he might have engaged in a pissing competition to show how informed he was, in an attempt to catch the other person off guard.

He wasn't in the mood for that now. Nor would it have helped the current operation. He had to remind himself that although China wasn't the enemy, they weren't an ally, either. But, they needed to work together.

"What about you?" she said, seeking to put the topic of conversation back on to him. "Did you ever serve in Afghanistan?"

It seemed a genuine question. The fact was he didn't feel uncomfortable around her. If anything, he still felt like he owed her a debt. Engaging in some mindless conversation was the least that he could do.

"Yep…several tours," he replied.

"What was it like?"

He gazed out of the window again. Even after all these years, he still didn't know how to answer that question. Sometimes it elicited positive thoughts of some of his best days in uniform, serving alongside men who he would forever consider his brothers. Other times all he could think about was the permanent scars it had left on him, obtained in a folly of a war that served no strategic purpose which had cost him some dear friends.

"Well, it was a war. They're never good," he said simply.

She could tell it was a topic he didn't particularly like talking about. Her own understanding in the studies of war, obtained through her political science degree from Peking University, gave her enough insight into the effects war had on soldiers.

"Confucius says: 'he who conquers himself is the mightiest warrior'," she said to him.

Kryton looked at her, impressed. His martial arts teachings had taught him that a man is never truly at peace until he finds peace within himself.

He smiled at her and looked back out the window.

She returned her attention to the notes in front of her. He glanced back at her out of the corner of his eyes.

*Another time. Another place – who knows*, he thought to himself.

He quickly turned his attention back to the task at hand.

"Who do you think was behind all this. The Russians perhaps?" he said, wildly speculating.

She shook her head.

"We don't believe so. There is no intelligence to support that. This is a group of actors that have, how do you say, 'gone off of the reservation'?"

He laughed at her accurate use of an American idiom.

"Yep. That's what it seems like."

"What will you do if you catch Wallis first?"

She shrugged her shoulders slightly.

"Well, everyone on the island is now looking for him. The fact is he tried to explode a bomb on an official Chinese government delegation. The Taiwanese will feel the same way."

She was right. Wallis wasn't now just wanted by the Americans.

Nothing in the five-eyes intelligence indicated Russian involvement, either. There would be no Edward Snowden like amnesty coming from any state actor. A guy selling a USB to a foreign intelligence service was one thing, but trying to assassinate the U.S. President was a completely different ball game. He was public enemy number one, and the U.S. was unlikely to stop hunting him down for anyone.

# 9

The small jet made its approach from the seaward side under the cover of darkness in the early hours of the morning. Hong Kong International Airport was still abuzz, despite a noticeable drop in international travel in the region due to the recent geopolitical events.

Tourists were sceptical that war wouldn't break out. Despite recent intelligence diminishing the chance of war between China and the U.S., who were now clandestinely working together, the public narrative was still one of potential conflict.

That's how the two superpowers wanted it. They wanted the attack planners to believe that they were still the hunters, when in fact, they were now being hunted.

Chen disembarked first, as protocol dictated, quickly followed by Kryton. No passports. No customs check. For all intents and purposes, Kryton wasn't even there.

A ghost in the night. A silent hunter.

He followed Chen into another SUV, and in a convoy of three cars they quickly departed the airport through a side gate and into the main thoroughfare leading to the North Lantau Highway.

The convoy rushed up the highway and towards the eastern side of Lantau Island.

Half an hour later, they had crossed the several bridges joining the various islands and were now on Hong Kong Island proper. The convoy moved through the minimal traffic with ease, soon pulling up to a warehouse in the Sai Wan district.

The SUV pulled up next to a guardhouse. The driver slightly lowered the window and had a brief conversation with one of the guards. He was dressed like a security guard from any given Western movie – the sheriff

43

like uniform, peaked cap, large utility belt around the waist and a raincoat. Just like a mall cop.

Except these weren't any ordinary mall cops. Kryton watched as one of the other guards stood by the passenger side of the SUV. As the guard turned slightly, Kryton observed a Chinese made QCW-05 submachine gun hanging from a shoulder sling at the side of the guard.

Kryton grinned slightly. Wherever this place was, it was well protected.

The guards opened the gate and the small convoy drove through. They proceeded down a darkened alley, turning into another side road before driving into the open roller door of one of the warehouses.

The convoy came to a stop inside the well-lit warehouse. Kryton followed Chen out of the car.

He stopped in his tracks as he observed a flurry of activity in the improvised operational centre now in front of him.

Essentially, it was a Chinese version of a SOCCE.

"Where are we?" he asked Chen.

He followed her as she walked to a small cubical that was possibly once used as the foreman's office.

"This is an MSS operational detachment. It's been set up for this particular operation."

*Cunning. Hiding in plain sight*, thought Kryton, noting that their SOCCE was in the middle of busy Hong Kong area, whilst his own sides was in a remote and highly secure military base in the middle of the Pacific Ocean.

Horses for courses.

The two walked into the small cubicle, where a middle-aged man was standing over a small table receiving a brief from what appeared to be a junior analyst. Kryton observed the many maps on the wall, as well as numerous images of Chinese workers standing under what appeared to be propaganda material. He assessed it was a machinery parts factory when not being utilised to chase traitors.

He saw several familiar images on the wall, all linked to each other and arranged like a pyramid. It was a network diagram – essentially an improvised chart showing how a group of people are linked. It had the Boss from Dili as well as his companions; the waiter from Taipei; as well as a few other official PLA portraits which Kryton assessed to be the other known lower members of the conspiracy.

At the top of the chart were several blank spaces.

These were the people they didn't know yet. The people they were in Hong Kong to locate and identify.

The man looked up, smiling broadly once he saw Chen.

She smiled back, walking over and shaking his hand. They engaged in some small talk in Mandarin before she turned towards Kryton.

"Colonel Yen – this is Zach Kryton of the Australian Army."

The man extended his hand, which Kryton shook respectfully. He noted the firm handshake, which wasn't usual in Chinese custom. Like many senior members of the MSS, Yen held a military rank. Kryton quickly appraised the man – more out of habit than because he considered him a threat. He was confident that the man could handle himself, if only from the handshake alone.

"It's nice to meet you, sir," Kryton said to him.

Yen said something to the analyst, who dutifully left the room.

"Please, have a seat," he said to the new arrivals, gesturing to some chairs around the table.

They sat down at a table that wouldn't have looked out of place in a 1970's suburban British home.

Yen proceeded to speak in English.

"We have analysed the intelligence you gained for us in Taipei. Beijing has confirmed that there has been a small element from a special operations unit from Guangzhou performing most of the tactical tasks in this conspiracy. That unit has now been confined to barracks and a full investigation is underway."

"What will that achieve, in the short term at least?" asked Kryton.

Yen turned in his seat to face Kryton more directly.

"Simple. Whoever is missing will be a suspect. We'll also question the other unit members to determine what they knew."

Kryton nodded. He had heard stories about communists purging entire military units for the indiscretion of a few members.

The young analyst returned to the room with a tray containing a pot of warm tea. He placed it down on the table before leaving again. Yen poured the tea into three small cups, serving them to Chen and Kryton.

He sat back down and took a sip.

"Okay," he commenced, "we have intelligence that a senior PLA officer, who is the head of the special unit assigned to the traitor you detained in Taipei, and of the men you unfortunately encountered in Dili, Mister Kryton, is meeting an unknown person later today."

"Who is he?" asked Chen.

45

The Colonel pulled out a folder from under some other papers and opened up a dossier. He removed an A4 sized picture and placed it in front of Chen and Kryton.

"This is Lieutenant-Colonel Wang Jianwu of the Guangzhou Military Region," he said as Chen and Kryton looked at the official photo of a man in full PLA uniform.

It's what ADF members called a 'death photo' – simply because the only time it ever got used was if you died in combat and they needed a photo to give to the media.

"Does he have any family?" asked Chen.

"No. Unlike the other members of this conspiracy, he has no family ties. His parents were killed in a factory accident when he was young, and he was raised by the state."

Kryton looked intensely at the photo. He saw a proud man, seemingly confident and with every opportunity for career advancement in front of him.

*Why would you betray your country?* he thought to himself.

"What about the families of the other traitors? Have we interrogated them?" asked Chen.

The tone of the question unsettled Kryton.

Cold and clinical.

He had to check himself for a moment and remember where he was, and the reputation of the people he was working with. This was the Chinese MSS, after all.

"We are questioning them, but we have no more information so far."

Kryton didn't want to think about just how that 'questioning' was being conducted.

"Where is this meeting occurring?" asked Kryton, trying to segue get back onto topic.

Yen stood up and cleared the table of the materials. Underneath was a map of Hong Kong, essentially acting as a table cloth.

"Here," he said, pointing at the Sha Tin Racecourse.

"The Hong Kong Jockey Club is holding the annual Hong Kong Trophy race day later today. It is one of the richest horse races in Asia," continued Yen.

Chen and Kryton looked over the map, taking in the information being briefed to them.

"Do we know where this guy is now?" asked Kryton.

46

"Thanks to the American NSA, our signals unit out there in the factory has the phone and sim card numbers known to be linked to Jianwu."

"That's all well and good, sir, but do we know where he is right now?" asked Kryton.

"No. We believe he is turning the phone off and only using it when needed."

"Well, do we know exactly where and at what time this meeting will take place?"

Yen shook his head before continuing to speak.

"We will have our agents stationed throughout the racecourse with their equipment. It's portable technology and easily concealed. We expect that Jianwu will have his phone with him and likely use it. If that phone, or any of the others that we have in the database enter the detection bubble, we'll be able to triangulate their positions. This should lead us to the target."

Kryton listened as the Colonel outlined the plan. He had seen in Afghanistan and Iraq an all too great a reliance on technology to find targets. His own training and experiences told him that nothing could beat a human source.

"Do you have other sources? I mean, how did you know about the meeting in the first place?"

Yen looked at his female colleague for a moment. Chen nodded softly.

"Yes, but it is not one hundred per cent confirmed. No intelligence is perfect," said Yen, seemingly affronted that Kryton was questioning their capabilities.

The Australian sensed this. He wanted to keep favour with his hosts.

"Sir, I understand that. I'm very impressed with how much you know, and I'm grateful to be here to work with you."

Yen seemed appeased by Kryton's humility.

"However, we don't know exactly *where* in the track the meeting is. We don't know what time and we're relying on them using their phones. And if that doesn't work, I suppose we'll just have to —"

"Walk all over the racecourse until we are lucky enough to find them," interjected Chen, slightly grinning.

"As the Colonel said, intelligence isn't perfect," she added.

Kryton slowly exhaled. He knew that the races at Sha Tin could attract tens of thousands of people, and the track was huge.

"That will take a lot of manpower," said Kryton.

"That, Mister Kryton, is something we can manage," said Colonel Yen, gesturing towards the door and out to the factory floor.

Kryton followed the two Chinese intelligence operators out onto the factory floor and into their operations bay. He was blown away with what he saw.

There were at least fifty people now milling around, all in small groups and being briefed over what appeared to be the same documents that Kryton had also just been briefed on.

"Holy shit," Kryton whispered under his breath.

*They're efficient, I'll give them that*, he also thought to himself.

Unlike in Australian intelligence circles, where resource restraints meant that surveillance teams and intelligence operators typically had to be flown around to support multiple operations, the MSS had a civil population of nearly one billion people to recruit from. That allowed them a workforce unmatched by any Western nations.

"These are all your people based in Hong Kong?" Kryton asked Chen.

"Umm, yes, I believe so. This is an important area for us," she said cheekily, knowing full well that the West already knew that is was.

Students protesting the dilution of democratic rights combined with Western nation intelligence agencies keeping tabs on one of the regions busiest trade hubs meant the MSS kept a close eye on the small former British enclave.

Kryton stood with Chen as Yen walked among the groups.

"The Colonel will give a full brief soon," she said.

Kryton nodded as he watched as the operators went about their business. For a moment, he felt like he was in the viper's den. He had to remind himself that, for now at least, they were playing on the same side. Chen excused herself and went off to talk to some of the other agents on the other side of the working area

Despite being amongst a group that would otherwise be an adversary, he could feel a familiar vibe. It was the sense of anticipation that came before setting out on an operation – even one that should simply be a basic surveillance activity.

He felt his fingers twitch, and for the first time in nearly twenty-four hours, he realised that he hadn't noticed that his body was aching. He was impressed with their set up, especially with what appeared to be a mobile operation. He noticed a small group of young operators standing over a table, cleaning and adjusting their weapons. He walked over to join them.

"G'day boys, mind if I join you?" said the much larger Australian, pulling his Sig Sauer from its concealed holster and slapping it down on the table.

The three smaller men looked up at the intruder, wide-eyed. One even jumped back a step.

"It's all good, mate," said Kryton, beaming a smile while reaching out to help the man with his balance.

One of the men said something to his companion in Mandarin. The companion shrugged his shoulders, indicating that he had no idea who this large Caucasian man was.

Kryton saw some plain white cleaning cloth and some oil. He took some and put it down in front of him, then expertly pulled his pistol apart and laid the pieces out neatly in front of him. He looked at the men, smiling.

One of them gathered up enough courage to talk to Kryton.

"American?" he asked, using what was a basic understanding of English.

Kryton shook his head.

"No. Australian."

The three men looked at each other, speaking quickly in Mandarin and appearing more at ease, nodding their heads furiously. Kryton tried not to laugh. They reminded him of Larry, Moe and Curly, but in a complementary way.

"I like…Tim Cahill," said the same man, smiling like a star-struck schoolboy, referring to the famous Australian soccer player.

"Ahhh, yeah, me too. He's pretty good!" said Kryton, motioning with his head as if he was putting one past the keeper for a goal.

He continued to clean his pistol, and in a few minutes, he had reassembled the weapon, tested its functionality, and placed it back in his holster.

Chen joined him at the table, explaining to his new friends who the foreigner was. They laughed, each shaking his hand. She motioned for Kryton to join her away from the table.

"They're young," he observed.

"Yes. We usually give our younger operators experience in mainland operations before they move further afield," she said.

Kryton nodded. It was a practice not too dissimilar to how most intelligence agencies worked – new recruits heavily supervised until they proved themselves.

"So, what is the basic plan? What do we do when we find this Lieutenant-Colonel?"

"I think you'll agree that this entire thing has been well funded and highly orchestrated. That means there are some well-placed and senior people involved."

Kryton nodded in agreement.

"We seem to have disrupted the lower levels, but we still need to know who was behind it all. We are hoping that Colonel Jianwu will lead us to them."

"The head of the snake," observed Kryton.

She looked up at him and smiled.

"Exactly. Perhaps we can even find your American traitor in the process," she said.

*I'd sure like to have that opportunity,* he thought to himself.

The two stood side by side for a moment, observing the hive of activity.

"Tell me," said Chen in a more relaxed tone, "is it true you stopped the missile attack on Air Force One by mere seconds?"

Kryton kept his eyes front for a second or two, then looked down at her with a grin.

"Who told you that?"

She averted her eyes for a moment and just shrugged, looking back at him curiously.

The fact was she could have made the assumption based on the myriad of media reporting on the incident.

"Just in the right place at the right time, I suppose," he said.

She shook her head.

"I think you have good chi, Mister Kryton. Let's hope it serves us today."

He nodded as she walked off. Maybe she was correct. Maybe it was the Chinese concept of chi, meaning a positive energy flow. Maybe it was karma. Maybe it was even luck. He'd saved the Presidential plane from the missile, stopped a bomb attack in Taipei, and, had come within milliseconds of being shot by Wallis.

The problem was, the threat was still out there. And luck wouldn't last forever.

# 10

The group of MSS agents sat in a neatly arranged square, facing an electronic screen at the front of the operations hub. Kryton sat next to Chen at the rear.

The audience stood as Colonel Yen stepped out of the office to give operational orders. He gestured for the mostly young operators to sit.

He commenced his brief, speaking Mandarin. The screen displayed various images of the detained members of the Guangzhou special forces unit.

"He's giving some background detail. Not everyone is completely aware of all the intelligence yet," Chen whispered into Kryton's ear.

The picture of Jianwu appeared on the screen.

The audience studied it astutely. This would be the target. They would need to be able to recognise him on sight. Potentially after only a quick glance or among a large crowd – which they would find at the track today.

Several images of the racecourse appeared on the screen, followed by numerous PowerPoint slides with all sorts of diagrams on them.

"He's discussing each team's part in the operation and their area of responsibility," whispered Chen, helping Kryton keep up with the brief.

He was impressed with the professionalism with which it was being conducted, and the level of detail, particularly since most of the intelligence had only recently been acquired.

Fortunately, Colonel Yen had already briefed Kryton into the wider operation, as well as the Australian's role in it, earlier. Kryton would lead a small component of English-speaking operators.

The surveillance teams would be divided up and be responsible for various areas of the racecourse. They would report to their team leader,

52

who would in turn report back to the operations hub where Colonel Yen would oversee the entire operation.

In the wings of the track in the surrounding streets would be a covert 'snatch and grab' team, ready to move if the target, or targets, were identified.

All seemingly simple, but then again, all plans are – until they're executed.

Colonel Yen concluded the brief and the teams dispersed to continue their final preparations. Each team would move to different locations, in various attire to allow them to blend in, and essentially just wait.

Two operators, both seemingly in their mid-twenties, came up to Kryton and introduced themselves.

Agent Chang, a stocky young man, and Agent Xiang, a petite but intimidating young woman, presented themselves to the Australian. They greeted him, almost in unison. They both spoke exceptionally good English.

Agent Chen said a few words to them in Mandarin, obviously detailing to them that they would be working for Kryton, and what her expectations would be.

"Shi," they both said, again in unison, giving the Mandarin for *yes*.

*Christ, she's given me a couple of robots,* Kryton thought to himself.

However, after a few minutes of talking to the two young agents, Kryton was pleased to discover that both of them had had experience abroad, although they didn't elaborate in detail as to what it involved. He was particularly pleased to discover that Chang had visited Australia as a student, and had taken up surfing.

"Do you still surf?" Kryton asked him.

"No. Unfortunately, there isn't much surfing in Hong Kong," said the young man.

Kryton could sense a longing in the tone of his voice, something only surfers deprived of their waves could truly understand.

"Alright. So, do you have any questions?" Kryton asked his team.

They both shook their heads. Xiang guided Kryton over to the back of one of the SUV's and helped him set up a covert portable radio. Each team would be on their own network, and Colonel Yen would control them all, passing information between teams as necessary. Separate networks amongst the individual teams would ensure brevity of information on the main network. It would be needed. Otherwise, a singular radio network for a surveillance operation of this magnitude could end up sounding like a pub during happy hour.

# 11

The barriers opened with a metallic thud, releasing the field of fourteen horses onto the luscious green grass. The thoroughbreds commenced their run down the back straight as the picturesque hills that contained the Mui Fa Ancient trail rose up in the background.

The fifth race would be a twelve-hundred metre sprint around the beautifully manicured track. The roar of the thirty-thousand plus crowd filled the air as eager punters watched as the horses that they had bet their hard-earned cash on thundered around the course.

Kryton stood amongst the crowd at the base of the main grandstand. The myriad variety of dress codes ensured that he and his team would fit in nicely amongst the throng of eager punters and racing enthusiasts.

"Chang, what's your location? It's impossible to move in here," he said into his covertly worn radio.

He moved among the bustling crowd, which by now was becoming even more excited as the field of horses made its way into the home straight.

"I have you in my sights, I'm several rows above you, next to the concourse entrance with the 'five' above it."

Kryton struggled to hear the reply as he turned to his left and looked up at an angle. He could see his new colleague, exactly where he said he was.

"Roger. And Xiang...location?"

"I'm along the same level, near concourse entrance seven," replied the female voice in his earpiece. Kryton scanned across to where she said she was, but the waving of arms and the general movement of the excited racegoers made it impossible for him to see her.

It didn't matter. He had radio contact as well as her location, and that was all he needed. Surveillance teams didn't always need to maintain visual contact. It was just sometimes reassuring to see a familiar face, though.

The cacophony of cheering, thundering hooves and the race caller over the public address system made it difficult for the team to hear each other.

*The Mighty Lancer* crossed the line by a half neck, thrilling the punters who had heavily backed the horse into pre-race favouritism. Kryton couldn't believe how packed it was at the track. He'd spent many Saturdays deep in the betting ring at Royal Randwick Racecourse back in Sydney, but even on the biggest race days there, it didn't seem as busy as it was now.

The crowd would be like a double-edged sword. It would make it easier to blend in and reduce the chance of being detected; however, it made it hard to stick to a target – that's if you can find it in the first place.

They'd been in location for a few hours, essentially just waiting for some information to come in from the technical teams who were relying on a phone to ping in their signals emission traps.

"Okay team, wait a second," he said to his two young Chinese subordinates.

He discreetly switched his radio to allow him to talk back to the operations hub. The radio had been set to ensure that he was still listening to any communications coming from there. It had been very quiet, suggesting that none of the other teams was having much luck.

"Base – this is Kryton. Can we get a status update, please?" he said politely into the radio.

Surveillance teams only spoke on the radio when they needed to, in order to maintain professionalism and to not clog up the radio network with unnecessary chatter which could disrupt a successful operation.

That didn't mean that there wasn't the occasional mention of a pretty girl passing a location or the use of some colourful language to express the frustration that often came with surveillance operations.

"This is base. No positive detection based on our technical means. Continue your visual search."

Kryton just shook his head. Waiting and hoping were all part of the game.

"Roger," he replied, before switching back to talk to his team.

"Nothing sighted yet, team."

Both of the young Chinese agents acknowledged the radio transmission. They had been on task for nearly six hours. Kryton was impressed by their professionalism to this point. The Chinese had a reputation for picking the best and brightest to join the MSS. Surveillance work could be highly demanding and tiring. It required constant alertness combined with extreme patience.

"Keep an eye out," he said simply to his team.

Kryton walked through the crowd at the base of the main grandstand and into the betting ring. Races from all over the world were being shown on large screen televisions, and punters were scanning the form guides seeking the next winner. Kryton allowed himself a moment to look up at the large electronic board with all the prices for the horses in the next race.

*Keep focused,* he thought to himself with a small smile.

For the next thirty minutes there was still nothing. Kryton made his way to the parading ring where the horses for the next race were being led around before the jockeys jumped on to take them onto the track proper. He made his way to a secluded area near a small brick building. He took out a small phone provided to him by Agent Chen. He dialled it.

"Yes?" came the voice over the other end.

She was still back at the operations hub with Colonel Yen. The phone would allow them to have a private, yet secure, conversation, as well as to take pictures and transmit the imagery back to the operations hub if needed.

"It's Kryton. What's happening?"

Chen stood behind the table where a small group of analysts were intently monitoring several small computer screens. Numerous electronic rings were overlayed on maps of the Sha Tin area, indicating much of the communications traffic occurring. These were connected to the covert mobile intercept stations being carried around by the MSS agents in and around the track.

They were just waiting for something to pop up.

"Nothing as yet. How are things out there?" she asked him.

Kryton had trouble hearing her, even though he was in one of the quieter parts of the track.

"Packed in like sardines here," he replied.

She frowned, unsure if she had heard him correctly. It was simply a misunderstanding of the idiom. Her silence made him realise that he should have been more general in his response.

"Busy. It's busy. We'll stand by," he said, ending the call.

The bugle call of 'call to the post' played over the loudspeaker, indicating that the next race would start in approximately ten minutes.

Kryton walked back towards the grandstand, joining thousands of people who were spilling out of the dining rooms, betting areas and bars to view the next race.

"Team – location check," he said into his radio.

"At north-east corner of the concourse," replied Chang.

"And Xiang?"

Silence. Once again, Kryton discreetly fiddled with his radio, ensuring the earpiece cord hadn't become loose.

"Xiang?" he said again, walking out onto the southern corner of the grandstand and onto the concourse which overlooked the home straight.

The radios were of good quality. It was possible she had moved into a heavily concreted area where the signal was disrupted. Kryton could hear Chang also trying to make contact, which was standard practice during lost communications.

Just as he thought he might have to go looking for her, a whisper came through the earpiece.

"Possible sighting of target, central grandstand," said Xiang.

Kryton's eyes darted across the concourse. He started walking briskly to where he assessed the young agent might be.

"Roger. I'm walking your way. Chang, hold at north-east corner," he instructed the two agents.

Kryton was now trying to walk against the flow of human traffic as he made his way across the concourse.

"I'm centre of the grandstand in vicinity of the executive suites. I'm certain I have eyes on target," said Xiang as she maintained the commentary to her team leader.

Kryton discreetly turned the radio talk switch over to the other channel.

"Base – possible sighting of target," he said.

"We acknowledge," came the quick reply.

The Australian moved across the concourse and made his way to the grandstand's lower levels. He could see the open-air corporate and executive suites, but from where he was standing, the crowd just appeared to be a blur.

"Xiang, where are you compared to target?"

"I am at the end of row seventeen. The target is in the third box from the southern end," she said.

Kryton now had an exact location, and slowly moved up into the open grandstand proper. He found a walkway in the middle and proceeded north towards the executive suites. In a few moments, he was now close enough that he could see individual faces. The rich and elite of Hong Kong's social set were in attendance.

He looked across the grandstand, seeking to visually locate his colleague.

"Xiang, prepare to adjust your hat…now," instructed Kryton.

The very specific but ordinary movement was enough to allow Kryton to identify the location of Xiang, sitting at the end of the row she had briefed him on, about thirty-five metres away from his location. Neatly attired in a light green dress with a brimmed hat and fascinator, she blended in nicely with the crowd.

"I have you," said Kryton.

Xiang lowered her head and pretended to play around with her handbag.

"Target is up to your left, about thirty metres away," she said quietly over the radio.

Kryton moved across the walkway to the back of one of the rows. He pulled the newspaper form guide out of the back of his jeans and pretended to look down at it as he turned to face the direction where the target should be.

The crowd raised to their feet and roared as the race caller announced the start of the race, blocking Kryton's view.

"Shit," he mumbled to himself as he attempted to get a better position.

Although he trusted that Xiang was in a good enough position to make a call on if the person she could see was actually the target, it required another operator to also make a visual contact before the grab team could be called in. They would aim to keep eyes on the target and follow them until they were in a less obvious location for the grab team to make their intercept.

He subtly moved closer to the executive suites, trying to get an image of the third one from the southern end. He observed as a hospitality waiter stood in front of a small group of men. The waiter was pouring from a bottle of champagne.

*C'mon, mate. Move*, Kryton thought to himself.

The crowd cheered as the horses continued along their journey, with the race caller getting more and more excited as they turned into the home straight.

The waiter, his back turned to Kryton, moved from his hunched over position, stood up, then walked off back up the stairs, exposing the two men he had previously obstructed from view.

Kryton squinted, trying to get a better view up through the moving crowd and into the executive suite from his current position.

There was no mistaking it. There, no more than about thirty-five metres in front of him, stood Jianwu. Dressed for the races in a neat grey suit with a black tie, he was standing next to an older, shorter Chinese man, cheering their horse home.

"Base – this is Kryton. Target confirmed. Executive suite three," he said succinctly into his radio.

"Acknowledge. Sending support to you now," came the reply.

Kryton removed his phone from his pocket, quickly manipulating its touch screen buttons and taking several snaps of the two men in quick succession. He immediately sent them through to the operations hub.

"That *is* Jianwu," said Chen to Yen, each looking at the images now displayed on the screens in front of them.

"Who is the other man?" she asked him, looking at the previously unseen figure.

Yen shook his head, unsure himself.

"Send this to Beijing," he said to one of his analysts, who nodded before sending the images to MSS headquarters.

The Chinese MSS had some very large files, particularly of anyone seen to be opposing the state or CCP rule.

Back at the track, Kryton guided Chang into a position at the top of the stairs of the grandstand in order to create a box around the two men. The crowd cheered as the wall of horses crossed the line. The race stewards would be needed to determine the actual winner in a photo finish.

Jianwu and the unknown man cheered together, confident that they had backed the actual winner. Kryton stayed in his position, leaning on the seats of the grandstand as the crowd started to move off again after the race. It was getting harder to see what was happening.

Kryton took a chance. He inched closer, seeking to maintain eyes on the target. He instructed Xiang to do the same. She was also having the same issue keeping a firm eye on them amongst the heavy crowd.

The unknown man reached into his pocket and pulled out an envelope, handing it to Jianwu. The special forces soldier's demeanour changed significantly. He looked down at the envelope then back at the man. He nodded, taking the envelope and placing it into his own coat pocket. The two men engaged for a few moments in what seemed like an intense conversation, before they shook hands. At that point, Jianwu turned and walked out of the suite, walking up the stairs and towards another walkway near the top of the grandstand.

"Chang, are you good to pick up and follow?" asked Kryton.

"Yes," replied the young man.

Kryton walked briskly to another flight of stairs parallel to the ones Jianwu had ascended. He raced up to them, seeking to get into a location where he could support Chang to follow Jianwu.

"Base – target is moving. My team is following," briefed Kryton to the operations hub.

"He mustn't have his phone with him. We're not receiving any signals," said Yen across the radio.

Kryton would have to ensure that his team stuck as close to Jianwu as they could. The other teams were spread all over the racecourse and it would take a while to get into a position to support them.

Kryton reached the top of the stairs, stopped and turned. He was now at an undercover walkway that led to the internals of the grandstand.

"Target is moving south," said Chang.

Kryton hugged the north wall. He knew that he was on the same level as Jianwu, so that meant that the Chinese officer was coming straight towards him. The Australian placed the newspaper in front of his face, peering over the top just enough to observe Jianwu walk past him, several metres away from where he was standing. He was heading towards another set of stairs.

A few seconds later, he watched as Chang also walked past him, maintaining the appropriate distance from the target to keep eyes on him, but not close enough to be compromised. It was a difficult task, considering the hordes of people moving about the congested area.

Just as Kryton was about to step out to follow Chang, he noticed two men in dark suits walk past his position, walking next to each other.

It didn't seem right. Everyone else was wearing a mixture of light coloured neat, business or plain casual clothing. These two looked like the Blues Brothers, inclusive of dark sunglasses. He held back for a moment, before stepping out to join the crowd and continuing to follow.

"Have you got anyone in support yet?" he asked the operations hub.

"Negative," came the reply.

"Acknowledge. It looks like he has a bodyguard team with him, to the rear and providing standoff cover," Kryton briefed back to Yen.

Kryton continued following, down the stairs to the rear of the grandstand and into the betting ring, which was now abuzz with punters still awaiting the result of the last race.

"Chang, you have company. Two bodyguards in dark suits, about five metres behind your position."

The young agent kept following Jianwu. Kryton was still descending the stairs, and could now see all of the men in staggered intervals in front of him amongst the crowd.

Jianwu proceeded to a betting window, handing over a ticket. Chang appeared confused by the sudden stop. He fiddled around with his hands for a moment, standing off to the side from where the target was.

"Pull your phone out and pretend you're on it," said Kryton.

Chang did so, but then took a few more steps towards Jianwu.

*Shit, you'll be able to smell his cologne from there,* Kryton thought to himself.

"Mate, stand off. You're too close," Kryton demanded into the radio, standing on the stairs above the betting ring so he could better see what was unfolding.

"I'm in the betting ring, I can change positions with him," said Xiang into the radio as she made her way to where Chang was.

Chang moved to stand back, but bumped into another patron who was carrying a tray of drinks. The tray went flying into the air as the poor middle-aged racegoer fell to the ground. The man shouted angrily in protest, his coat and tie now drenched in beer.

The noise attracted the attention of the bodyguards, as well as Jianwu who was pocketing his winnings as he left the counter of the betting window. Chang instinctively reached down to help the man up, but then mistakenly looked up quickly.

He made direct eye contact with Jianwu and stared at him for a moment. The startled but intense look on Chang's face told the army officer that something was not right. He looked at his bodyguards – one of who then started to close in on the young agent.

Chang, whether from fear or inexperience, saw the bodyguard getting closer and reached into his jacket to remove his concealed pistol.

"Oh no," Kryton said audibly to no-one in particular. He started moving quickly to get closer to help Chang. The crowd blocked his path, forcing Kryton to have to shove people out of the way.

No more than twenty-five metres away, the bodyguards had already sprung into action. The one closer to Jianwu rapidly ran towards his client, grabbing him and using his own body as a shield and trying to remove him away from the area – a job made all the more difficult due to the crowd.

The other guard leapt in front of Chang, drawing his own pistol and pointing it directly at the MSS agent. The two men stood in a Mexican standoff for a few seconds as Kryton desperately tried to reach them.

"Shoot the prick," he shouted directly at Chang.

The two Chinese men kept shouting at each other in Mandarin, startling the nearby crowd. A woman screamed on seeing the two men pointing weapons at each other. This caused a mild panic, as racegoers started to run from the area.

Kryton was struggling to get through the hordes of people now desperately trying to go the other way. He sidestepped an elderly couple, inching closer. A clear path now presented itself, and he was now less than five metres from the bodyguard.

He sprinted the last few steps, launching himself shoulder-first into the short but stocky man. Both men went tumbling to the ground, landing on the concrete floor and causing Kryton's already damaged ribs to bring him even more pain.

The bodyguard also fell awkwardly, dropping his pistol. He quickly turned to his side, trying to determine what had just happened. He saw Kryton lying a few feet from him. He tried to reach out for his pistol, but Kryton dived at it and knocked it away. The two men grabbed each other whilst still on the ground, engaging in a grappling duel.

Kryton successfully managed to get on top of his opponent, who reached up at the Australian's face, forcing Kryton's head back. He turned to his left, causing the bodyguard to release his grip. He parried the man's arm away, exposing his face. Kryton rained two quick blows in succession down on the man's nose, the second of which broke it.

Kryton then adjusted his position, drawing himself up onto his knee, pulling the man's upper body up off the ground, creating enough space for himself to spin around onto his back, grabbing the man in a rear-naked choke with his legs wrapped around the helpless bodyguard's stomach.

Chang looked down at the two of them. Kryton looked back up at Chang. He couldn't believe that he was just standing there.

"For fuck's sake, go after them," he shouted to the young agent as the bodyguard continued to groan as Kryton continued to wrap him in an increasingly tightening grip.

Chang looked over his shoulder as Agent Xiang arrived. She said something in Mandarin, which stirred Chang into action. He sprinted off after Jianwu and the other bodyguard.

By now, a small crowd had gathered to watch the unfolding fracas. Two policemen, blowing their whistles loudly, arrived at the scene, dispersing some of the spectators. One pulled out his pistol, pointing it at the two men on the ground. Xiang stepped in, quickly talking to the other officer and discreetly showing him an I.D. card.

The bodyguard let out a last whimper as he passed out. Kryton released his choke. Xiang and the officer reached down to help move the unconscious bodyguard off of Kryton, helping him to his feet. He nodded at the officer in thanks, before grabbing the arm of Xiang and quickly departing the scene.

"Are you okay?" she asked him as they lightly jogged towards the exit.

Kryton held his ribs. They hurt like hell again from the fall.

"Yeah, I'll be fine," he said, breathing heavily.

He moved with Xiang to a small empty space near the entrance where the first aid office was situated. It was empty.

"Base – compromise, compromise, compromise," he said as Xiang looked over his head, where a small cut obtained in the struggle was bleeding.

"We understand, the grab team has been deployed," came the voice of Colonel Yen over the radio.

Xiang ripped open a first aid kit on the wall and grabbed a small gauze pad, handing it to Kryton.

"I'll be fine. Let's go," he said to her as he quickly pushed the pad onto the cut on his head.

The two of them ran out of the room and back into the entrance area of the track.

"Chang, where are you?" Kryton asked into the radio.

"Heading south-east parallel to Tai Po Road. I'm running –"

The transmission was interrupted by three quick pops, followed by two others. Kryton could hear them above the noise of the crowd, suggesting that the shots came from nearby.

64

A groaning whimper then came across the radio.

Kryton sprinted up the street along the front of the track, quickly followed by Xiang.

The screams combined with the sight of people quickly running in the other direction told Kryton that he was close to Chang's location. Kryton and Xiang ran up the road for another sixty metres, their pistols drawn and ready to engage any targets.

Lying to the side of the road, next to a flower bed near the entrance to the bus and VIP parking area, was Chang. He was bleeding from the shoulder, hit by one of the bodyguard's bullets. Less than twenty metres further up the road, sprawled across the gutter and lifeless, was the second bodyguard.

Chang's bullets had hit their target.

Kryton crouched down, looking over the injured man's head and looking for Jianwu.

"I'm sorry, sir," said the young man in between deep breaths.

Kryton looked over Chang's injuries. The bullet had gone in through his left shoulder and straight out the other side. Fortunately, it had only hit muscle, and not the bone or joint.

"It's okay, mate, you did well," Kryton reassured him as he placed Chang's free hand on the wound.

Xiang arrived, also crouching down next to them.

"He's fine, but he's going into shock," he briefed her.

She quickly pulled a scarf out of her handbag, folding it over to form an improvised bandage and placing it over Chang's wound. She spoke quietly to him in Mandarin. She must have tried to tell him a joke, because Chang started laughing, which caused him to start coughing.

Kryton stood up, looking ahead and into the car park. The commotion of two men yelling caught his eye. He looked to his slight left and saw Jianwu pulling a man out of the driver's side of a black Audi.

"He's over there, stay here," he shouted at Xiang as he sprinted after the target.

Kryton ran towards where the car was, hurdling another flower bed then hauling himself over a pedestrian railing. The sound of screeching tyres echoed across the small car park as Jianwu floored the luxury car. He drove out towards Kryton, seeking to go out from the direction he had just come in. Kryton dived out of the way as the black car flew around the corner, blocked in by the pedestrian railing.

Jianwu was forced to follow the road around next to the railing, now heading back towards the track. He soon found what he was looking for – the car park entrance.

"Shit," said Kryton, jumping back to his feet.

He looked around, scanning the car park to assess his options.

As he watched Jianwu speed off through the entrance, he noticed a silver-grey Lexus slowly reversing out of its bay near the same spot Jianwu had stolen his car from.

Kryton sprinted over to the car, reefing open the driver's side door.

"Out, out," he screamed at the bewildered elderly man looking back up at him.

The man and his female companion, probably his wife, leapt out of the car in fear as Kryton jumped in behind the wheel. He quickly looked over his shoulder to ensure there wasn't a baby or a young child in the back seats, before manoeuvring the car into the car park road and screaming off towards the entrance.

Several well-dressed racegoers were forced to jump for their lives as Kryton expertly drove the Lexus out of the entrance and into the slipway leading onto the streets of Hong Kong.

He sped around a small Hilux truck, receiving a loud disgruntled honk of the horn from the driver for his efforts. He was now driving parallel to the racecourse and could see the black Audi up in the distance.

Kryton floored the accelerator of the heavy automatic car, knowing that he had a disadvantage in the make and model compared to the lighter and more agile Audi.

"C'mon, you bitch," he said to the car as his foot hit the floorboard.

He could see Jianwu weaving in and out of the relatively light Sunday afternoon traffic.

*This guy has some skills*, Kryton thought to himself.

He reached down to ensure that the radio was still attached to his body, unsure if it had survived the dive to avoid being hit by the speeding Audi back in the car park. It had.

"Base – in pursuit of target, heading west along the racecourse."

"What road are you on?" came the reply.

Kryton looked down at the large screen in the middle of the dashboard. Fortunately, the electronic navigation map was on and working.

Unfortunately, however, all the words were in Mandarin.

Kryton rolled his eyes in frustration as he started pressing all the buttons on the touch screen, trying to keep one eye on the road to keep up with Jianwu.

First, the radio started playing. The next touch made it start playing some sort of Chinese classical music on the CD player.

"Shit," Kryton screamed, slapping the steering wheel and ignoring the screen to instead just focus on the road.

"I don't know, I'm just heading west. I'm in a silver-grey Lexus, target is ahead of me in a black Audi," he said on the radio.

"Okay, maintain the pursuit, we'll seek to vector support to you," came the voice of Agent Chen back over the radio.

Kryton continued the chase. He smiled at the thought that Jianwu must be asking lots of questions. Thirty minutes ago, he was comfortable enough to be in public having a good time with whoever that other man was. Now, however, he was speeding through the Hong Kong traffic, running from a Western operative who, after all that had occurred in the past few weeks, would stop at nothing to find out who was behind all of this.

And right now, the next piece of that puzzle was tearing through the open highways of outer Hong Kong.

# 12

Jianwu managed to find a slipway leading onto the main highway. He weaved in and out of the traffic, seeking to get as far away from Kryton as possible, as quickly as possible.

Kryton followed him up onto the slipway. He also had to weave his way through the traffic.

Both cars struggled to maintain any momentum, their speeds being bled by the slightest alterations in course that were required to move through the traffic.

Kryton knew his Lexus had a weight disadvantage over the lighter Audi, which would be able to manoeuvre on the road with greater ease.

They crossed the bridge over the Shing Mun River – the revving engines attracting the attention of the group of fishermen on the banks below. They continued at speed up the road, passing under a large green road direction sign.

"I'm on Sha Tin Road," Kryton said into the radio, grateful that the lasting legacy of British colonialism were road signs written in Mandarin *and* English.

Less than two minutes later, Jianwu noticed the traffic becoming heavier. He looked around, seeking an alternate route. There were none. He continued driving, soon noticing the cause of the slowing traffic.

He passed under another sign, this one saying 'Lion Rock Tunnel'. He moved past a small minibus, finding some clear space and an open lane. He could see up in front of him a row of toll booths, with cars neatly queuing and waiting to pay the toll. He noticed an empty lane to the far right. He manoeuvred over into it and noticed that it led to a boom gate covering any access past the booth.

He lined his car up directly with the boom gate.

He pushed down hard on the accelerator, almost ploughing it through the firewall. The Audi crashed through the wooden boom gate with a loud bang, sending shards of wood flying everywhere.

The commotion scared the life out of the poor toll booth worker sitting in her box counting the day's takings. She opened the sliding window and stuck her head out to see what the hell had just happened.

Kryton was not far behind. He followed Jianwu into the open lane just in time to see the black car crash through the gate. He grasped the steering wheel tightly, gritting his teeth in anticipation of driving the Lexus at speed through the narrow space.

His eyes widened when he saw the lady stick her head out of the booth. He smashed down on the horn in just enough time for the lady to turn her head the other way. She gasped as she saw a silver-grey car coming straight at her, headlights flashing and the horn sounding.

She ducked her head back into the booth just as Kryton tore through the narrow space. His speed created a wind tunnel, causing the papers and documents on her counter to go flying.

Kryton noticed a sign as he entered the tunnel in pursuit of Jianwu.

"Through the toll booth, I'm headed into Kowloon area, still behind the target," he said into the radio.

*Jesus, this is crazy*, he thought to himself as he continued the chase.

He knew he had to keep up with and not lose sight of the target. Jianwu was headed into one of the densest urban areas on the planet. Wallis had managed to escape, so this guy might be the only tangible link to finding who was behind this whole thing. If he managed to escape too, they may never know who was behind it.

It was going to prove difficult. The tunnel was a dual carriageway, but very tight with almost no room on the sides of the two lanes. Kryton looked down at his speedometer. He was teetering on one-hundred kilometres per hour. He exhaled deeply. This was scary driving. One tiny mistake could see him crash into the walls of the tunnel or another car, hurtling him up the tunnel as if he were in a pinball machine

Kryton continued up the tunnel, weaving between cars and narrowly avoiding a motorcyclist who was about to try and overtake another car before realising the danger at the last moment.

A minute later, Jianwu exited the tunnel, closely followed by Kryton. It had been a miracle that no one had been killed so far.

That luck was soon to run out.

Jianwu sped along the road as it led into the residential areas, the Australian still on his tail. The road was still a dual carriageway, and the traffic was beginning to become heavier as they got closer to Hong Kong proper.

A green taxi attempted to pull out into the right-hand lane to overtake a slower-moving car. Jianwu smashed on his car's horn. The sound alerted the taxi driver, who in his panic swiftly veered back to the left whilst hitting the brakes. This caused a van behind him to crash into his rear, causing a chain reaction that resulted in several cars crashing into each other.

"Shit," said Kryton as he sped up to get past the carnage, but not before several boxes of fruit became dislodged from a small truck, falling into Kryton's path. Fruits and vegetables went flying as Kryton crashed through the falling goods, covering his car in a mushy mixture that would not make it to the markets.

He turned on the windscreen wipers, trying to remove the mess from his windscreen. It was enough to clear his vision, and he could see Jianwu still trying to make his escape, now only thirty metres in front of him.

"Base – where the hell are you?" he shouted into the radio.

There was no immediate reply.

Kryton continued to chase Jianwu. The buildings were becoming noticeably taller as the two cars screamed into the most populated part of Hong Kong.

A moment later, Chen's voice came over the radio.

"We have a helicopter airborne. Five minutes," she said.

He knew that the helicopter would be of little to no help. At most, it could vector other teams onto the cars, but that would be near impossible to do among the myriad of high-rise buildings they were now approaching.

Jianwu knew what he was doing. He would easily be able to blend in amongst the population. Kryton couldn't let him get out of sight.

The special forces officer suddenly veered left, moving down a slipway off of the highway and into the back streets. Kryton followed, cutting off several cars in the process.

Jianwu was now tearing down the backstreets, still moving quite fast even though the roads were narrow. The chase continued past a school, over another road and past a Buddhist temple. A boys' soccer team scattered as Jianwu raced over a zebra crossing, sending several of their practice balls flying into the air. Kryton honked his horn, alerting the young players that there was still danger.

One of the players threw a ball at Kryton's car in anger as it passed them. It bounced harmlessly off of the rear passenger door.

"Don't blame you, mate" Kryton mumbled as he continued after Jianwu.

The narrow back streets slowed the Audi, allowing Kryton to draw even closer. People were forced to jump for their lives as the two luxury cars ripped through the confined area.

They went up a hill, slightly getting airborne as they raced over the crest. Jianwu swerved, narrowly avoiding a construction worker holding up a handheld 'slow down' sign. He crossed the marked lines, veering onto the other side of the road, forcing oncoming traffic onto the footpath. A red hatchback careered off of the road and into a bus stop, knocking the wooden structure over.

The magnificent view across Kowloon Bay opened up as they reached the foreshore. Jianwu applied the handbrake, performing a sharp ninety-degree turn before releasing the handbrake and flooring the accelerator.

Kryton followed him, reefing on the steering wheel while expertly manipulating the brake and accelerator pedals. It had been a while since he had completed his evasive driver training on the raceways and skidpans back in the Gold Coast Hinterland, but the muscle memory was still there.

The chase continued along the foreshore, speeds varying based on the congestion of the road. Jianwu kept looking over his shoulder, and each time the silver-grey Lexus would be right there behind him.

The two cars approached a set of traffic lights. Cars were backed up, and the road was blocked. Jianwu drove up onto the footpath, narrowly missing a young family, but running into a small vendor's cart, smashing it up and sending small trinkets, postcards and other small souvenirs all over the concrete.

Kryton followed, continually honking his horn to warn the pedestrians. He followed Jianwu back onto the street. The two were now driving the wrong way up the road, forcing the oncoming traffic to swerve out of the way.

Jianwu spun the steering wheel to the left, guiding his Audi up another side street, now once again parallel to the foreshore. Kryton could see a long trail of liquid spilling from underneath Jianwu's car. The punctured fuel tank slowed the Chinese man's momentum. Kryton pushed even harder on the accelerator, aiming straight for the rear of the Audi.

The two cars bumped with a loud metallic bang. Kryton looked down at the steering wheel in terror, having forgotten that the action might inflate the driver's side airbag. Fortunately, it didn't. He breathed a sigh of relief as he followed Jianwu up the same road. They were now between two large buildings, racing towards a main street.

Jianwu threw all caution to the wind, racing out of the narrow street and onto a main road running at an adjacent angle. His eyes widened as he crossed onto the road and into the path of a large garbage truck. He attempted to evade the truck by turning the steering wheel, but at his current speed all that he managed to achieve was to fishtail the Audi around, forcing it to crash into a heavy steel barrier on the side of the road.

Kryton saw the crash before he too was forced to apply the handbrake suddenly to avoid hitting several pedestrians that had blindly stepped in front of his path in order to watch the unfolding drama. The Lexus was still moving, so he spun the steering wheel to the right and drove the nose into the side of the building, coming to a sudden halt.

This time, the airbag did inflate, knocking Kryton's head back into the seat rest. He let out a groan, his nose once again suffering a painful blow. He grabbed at the bag, seeking to deflate it. The right-hand side was blocked by the wall, so Kryton climbed over the passenger seat and stumbled out of the car.

Two young university students with backpacks helped him to his feet, asking him if he was okay. Kryton looked down at them, nodding his head. He looked to his right and over the other side of the road. He could see a small crowd standing around the damaged Audi, Jianwu in the front seat desperately trying to restart the engine.

"Base – I've crashed near Kowloon Bay. I'm at –"

He paused and turned to one of the students.

"Where am I?" he asked the young man.

The students looked at each other bewildered, before looking back at Kryton. One of the students pointed up at a luxurious looking building across the street.

"That's the Chelsea Hotel," he said.

Kryton nodded.

"Thanks, kid."

He started walking across the road.

"In vicinity of the Chelsea Hotel," he briefed the operations hub.

Jianwu looked up over the steering wheel. Through the cracked windscreen he could see Kryton closing in. He gave up on the car and rapidly exited the driver's side, knocking over a shop attendant who, having come outside to see what was going on, was simply trying to help the driver of the crashed car.

Jainwu ran off up the street, pushing people aside as he headed back in the direction of the foreshore. Kryton sprinted across the street, avoiding a cyclist and jumping over the pedestrian barrier.

Jianwu tuned into a narrow single lane road, heavily bordered by retail shops. The pedestrian traffic was heavy, and Kryton had trouble keeping a visual sight of his target. Jianwu stumbled over a shop attendant who walked onto the footpath carrying a trolley laden with bags of rice. This gave Kryton just enough time to close the gap somewhat. Jianwu quickly got to his feet, sprinting up the footpath and towards an intersection.

He darted across the road, forcing buses and cars to brake suddenly. The sound of screeching tyres and car horns forced the pedestrians to stop and turn their heads. Several people even pulled out mobile phones in anticipation of filming something perhaps worthy of posting on their social media sites.

A few moments later, Kryton entered the same intersection, turning his head rapidly to watch for any traffic as he crossed the busy intersection. He was soon across it and could see Jianwu less than thirty metres in front of him, running into an undercover bus station.

The Australian increased his pace.

"Base – I'm in the bus station," he said into the radio, not exactly sure which one it was but certain that the operations hub would have an idea based on his last location update.

He came to a set of stairs and quickly ascended them, two steps at a time. Once at the top, he watched as Jianwu went running across a pedestrian overpass, situated above a main road. The Chinese man weaved his way through a large tourist group, pulling one of them down to the ground in an attempt to block Kryton who was closing in rapidly. Kryton easily managed to move around the poor tourist and continued the chase.

The beautiful sight of Victoria Harbour and its glistening blue water presented itself as Kryton reached the end of the overpass. He was now at the top of another set of stairs. He could see Jianwu about halfway down, seemingly starting to limp.

*Got you now, you bastard*, Kryton confidently thought to himself as he quickly descended the stairs.

Jianwu reached the bottom and quickly turned left, running along the brick walkway that bordered the waterline. Kryton gave chase, exerting himself for one final effort. He moved to the left, closer to the road, seeking to block any escape by Jianwu across the busy road. The operator lined the Chinese officer up from three metres, heaving his body shoulder first into the suited man.

The two soldiers went tumbling onto the brickwork, nearly knocking over a young couple who were taking a romantic walk along the foreshore. Jianwu was first to his feet, having almost somersaulted back upright from the shoulder charge. He looked down, seeing the cause of his tumble. He lunged at Kryton, seeking to grab his pistol from its holster.

Kryton pulled Jianwu down on top of him, forcing the Chinese man to have to place his arms out to stop the fall. Kryton grabbed him around the back of the neck, attempting to wrap his legs around the suited man and into a guard. Jianwu steadied himself with his other leg, splaying it out to the side of his body to prevent been caught in the guard. Instead of going for the pistol, he laid two clean punches into Kryton's ribs.

"Argghhh," screamed Kryton.

The pain from the two blows onto his existing injuries was excruciating. He turned to his side, smashing his forearm across Jianwu's face, forcing his head back. Kryton shifted onto his back once again, using the space he had now created to land a clean follow up punch to Jianwu's chin, causing him to see stars.

Kryton grabbed him by the shoulders, twisting the man's body and pushing it off of him. This allowed Kryton room to get onto his haunches and stand up.

Jianwu crawled over to the railing next to the waterline, using the metallic barrier to get back to his own feet. He steadied himself once he was up, turning to look at Kryton. He rubbed his jaw and gritted his teeth.

Kryton stood several feet away. He drew his pistol and pointed it straight at Jianwu.

"Get the fuck down," he shouted.

The Chinese man just looked straight back at him, fury in his eyes. He started walking briskly towards Kryton.

"Don't do it," said Kryton firmly.

Jianwu kept closing.

"Shit," mumbled Kryton as he took a few steps back, quickly holstering his pistol as Jianwu kept closing.

He knew they needed him alive, so shooting the man was not an option. Additionally, the 'just shoot him in the leg' approach only worked in the movies. A small crowd had already gathered, and a bullet could easily ricochet off a bone and into an innocent person.

Jianwu started running at the Australian, and when he was within arm's reach he launched a head high punch. Kryton easily ducked it, slightly bumping Jianwu and using the attacker's momentum to force him off balance. Like a flash, Kryton turned to face Jianwu, kicking the man front on clean in the stomach. This made him buckle over, and Kryton quickly followed up with an uppercut, forcing Jianwu's head back, and causing blood to start streaming from his nose.

The two men were of equal size and stature. Jianwu stumbled back, but quickly gained his footing. He brushed his hand over his nose and looked back at Kryton, even angrier than before.

*Oh crap*, thought Kryton to himself, wondering how his two clean blows hadn't felled his opponent.

Jianwu once again walked towards Kryton. The Australian raised his arms, ready for another go. Jianwu closed the gap, launching his own front kick at Kryton, who stepped back to avoid the blow. However, as quick as a striking snake, Jianwu followed it with a devastating rear kick with his opposite leg, which knocked Kryton back into the railing.

Jianwu attempted a quick flurry of punches, all blocked by Kryton who covered his body, taking the blows on his arms. He struck up at Jianwu's throat with his palms, both facing upwards and held together as if he was holding a small bowl.

This simple yet effective strike sent Jianwu flying backwards, coughing and spluttering. Kryton took a quick pace forward, landing three consecutive blows on his nose, forcing Jianwu to stumble back even further. The Australian launched himself at his opponent once again, grabbing him around the waist and forcing them both to crash into a flower bed. Kryton landed on top of Jianwu and was now in the full mount. He rained several blows down across Jianwu's face, who struggled in a vain attempt to cover his head.

Kryton stopped the attack, crossing his arms at the wrist and grabbing the back of Jianwu's coat collar, pulling up on his head and slightly turning his wrists at the same time. The move created a vice, trapping Jianwu's neck between his own collar and Kryton's wrists, cutting off the blood to his brain, strangling him. The Chinese man spluttered for a second or two, before passing out in Kryton's grip.

He held it for a moment, before releasing it and gently laying the Chinese man's head down on the neatly cut foliage. He needed the man alive. If he maintained the strangle for too long, he could end up killing him.

Kryton leaned back into a kneeling position. He suddenly realised how heavily he was breathing. He looked around. His intense gaze was enough to scare a few of the spectators away. He took in several deep breaths, trying to lower his heart rate.

He heard the sound of screeching tyres and emergency service sirens drawing closer. Additionally, the chopping sound of helicopter rotors was now also coming closer.

"Here comes the cavalry," he said softly.

Just as he was about to stand up, he remembered the transaction between Jianwu and the other man back at the racecourse. Kryton quickly hunched down next to his unconscious opponent, reaching into the coat pocket. He pulled out a small envelope. The same one Jianwu had received from the unknown man. It was thick and bulging.

He looked up as he ripped the top open. It was filled with U.S. dollars. On first glance, Kryton assessed there to be about ten-thousand dollars in hundred-dollar bills. He quickly flicked through the notes. He also noticed a small square device. He pulled it out.

It was an SD card, the type used for electronic data file transfers and storage.

Kryton thought for a moment. He placed the envelope back in the man's coat pocket, but discreetly put the SD card in the small pocket at the top of his jeans.

He sat back as several police cars came to a screeching halt on the road a few metres away. Kryton looked up, suddenly noticing that the flower bed he was sitting in contained a life-sized statue. He laughed when he saw who the statue was of.

"Not a bad effort, wouldn't you say Master Lee?" he said out loud as he stood up, using the base of the statue of martial arts legend Bruce Lee to help himself to his feet.

The police officers came running to where he was standing, their pistols drawn and yelling at him in Mandarin. Kryton looked at them submissively, putting his own hands up by his side.

The officers' attention was quickly drawn to the several dark SUVs that suddenly arrived on the scene. Scores of darkclad Chinese agents poured out. One of them was Agent Xiang. She spoke briefly to the head police officer, who quickly directed his officers to remove the civilians from the area.

A moment later, a dark helicopter arrived overhead. The pilot skilfully manoeuvred into a clear position on the now cleared road, placing the chopper down just metres from the street light poles.

The side doors of the helicopter opened. Agent Chen and Colonel Yen both disembarked, running over the where Kryton was standing next to two police officers, his hands still in the air.

Chen said something in Mandarin to the two young officers, showing them her I.D. card. Their eyes widened and they nodded respectfully, quickly running back to their cars.

Kryton lowered his hands and exhaled deeply.

"Are you okay?" asked Chen as she arrived by his side.

Kryton stepped out of the garden bed.

"Yeah," he said. "Just taking a tour of the city."

Chen couldn't help but laugh at the joke, especially considering the circumstances.

The two watched as several of the agents came over to retrieve Jianwu, who was now starting to rouse. They hauled him roughly across the road and into one of the SUVs.

"We have to leave here…now," she said.

Kryton nodded. Although Chinese authorities were very efficient in controlling the media and distribution of information, it was much harder to do in Hong Kong, where people were still well connected into Western social media.

He followed Chen back to the helicopter, ducking his head as they moved under the rotors. Less than a minute later, they were airborne. Kryton took a moment to take in the view as the helicopter traversed the beautiful Victoria Harbour.

Chen handed him a bottle of water. Kryton nodded in thanks, placing the bottle to his lips. He drank the entire half litre in almost one gulp, keeping a small bit to wash over his face. He quickly checked himself over for injuries. There was nothing permanent, just more sore ribs and perhaps a small loss of pride. He could live with that.

The helicopter raced across the harbour just above sea level – low enough that they could see the surprised expressions on the faces of the mostly recreational boat users enjoying a Sunday afternoon on the water.

Several minutes later, the pilot descended, landing on a small oval in Sandy Bay. There were two SUVs waiting for the chopper's passengers.

Kryton followed the two Chinese MSS staff into the lead car, where they proceeded to return to the operations hub.

# 13

Agent Xiang quietly placed her radio back into its hardened case, closing the lid and picking it up, walking it from the table she was working on to the back of one of the SUVs.

"Here, you might need this one, too," said a voice from the side of the car.

She looked up to see Kryton looking at her, holding up his own radio – neatly deconstructed and placed in a small box. She smiled at him, looking relieved.

"Oh… I was wondering where that one was," she said, taking the box from him.

"How are you feeling?" he asked her sincerely.

She turned around and sat up on the tail of the SUV. She shrugged her shoulders.

"First time seeing action?" he asked her.

She tilted her head to the side, smiling in an effort to conceal the fact she was still shaking – the body's natural reaction that occurs once the adrenalin wears off.

She looked at him and finally nodded.

"Yes."

He moved in to sit next to her on the SUV, nodding in empathy.

"Before I joined the army, I was a school teacher. The first time a bullet went over my head, I almost pleaded with God to trade the small creek I was lying in for a classroom – even if it was with the worst kids in the worst school," he said, laughing.

She looked up at him, disbelieving that the strong man next to her had ever felt fear.

"It's natural to be scared. Don't think less of yourself for it. It does get easier, but that sense of fear doesn't go away. And you don't want it

79

to. It's what keeps you from doing stupid things that might get you killed."

She nodded her head softly and smiled. He looked up, seeing Agent Chen waving him over from the small office. He jumped off of the SUV and took a few steps before turning around.

"You did well today. Chang will live. Your parents would be proud. You should be proud!" he said to her, trying to leverage a small part of Chinese culture that placed a high value on familial approval.

She looked at him, a beaming smile on her face.

He winked at her and turned, walking off to the office.

Colonel Yen was on the phone having an animated conversation with someone in Mandarin. Kryton moved to the corner of the office where Chen was looking over some documents.

"All good?" he asked her.

She closed the folder and looked up.

"Beijing isn't happy with the mess that was caused this afternoon," she said bluntly, looking at him.

He looked over at Yen, then back at her.

"Oh…I'm sorry!?"

She tried not to laugh.

"It's okay. Media is reporting that it was a local criminal organisation fighting amongst itself, so no harm will come from it."

"So, what's all that for?" he asked, gesturing towards Yen.

"Someone has to get yelled at," she said.

He nodded his head. He knew all too well how that worked. Even when you were in the right, you were wrong. Standard intelligence and military bureaucracy.

Yen finished the call and placed the receiver in its casing. He loudly said some words in Mandarin, which Kryton assumed were probably colourful in nature.

"Look, Boss, I'm sorry if I caused you –" Kryton started saying before Yen raised his hand to cut him off.

The Colonel just smiled, gesturing for the both of them to sit down.

"It's fine. We got what we needed. I appreciate your efforts, and will personally seek to make that representation to your embassy," he said.

"For now," he continued, "here's what we know. Beijing has analysed the pictures you transmitted from Sha Tin. The man with Colonel Jianwu is named Jieng Wang. He's an arms dealer, and was formerly a high-ranking member of the Party Congress," briefed Yen, referring to one of the highest levels in the Chinese Communist Party.

"Formerly?" said Kryton.

"Yes. He was removed two years ago. His ideas were…no longer in line with party values," said Yen, reluctant to give too much information away.

Kryton nodded, respecting that Yen was already sharing much more than would ever usually occur. They would now, though, because any intelligence gathered would be run through five-eyes databases, and might help get a better understanding of what was going on.

"So, where is he now?"

"Mister Wang and Colonel Jianwu are currently on their way back to Beijing where they will face some detailed interrogation," said Agent Chen.

*I'd hate to be them*, thought Kryton to himself, knowing that the two men would likely end up in a forced labour camp in the outer Chinese desert by the end of the week – *if* they were lucky.

Yen looked at Kryton.

"Did Jianwu have anything on him when you detained him?" he asked.

Kryton shook his head.

"No, I didn't check. Sorry. Why, what did you find?"

"We didn't find anything, either," replied Chen.

Kryton kept a straight face. He knew *he* was lying, but he wasn't sure if *they* were lying, too. Either they were lying by not telling him about the large sum of money that was in the envelope in Jianwu's pocket, or they didn't actually know about it and a now a dodgy MSS agent would be taking his family on a very nice holiday later in the year.

Kryton could sense the suspicion, but it didn't feel palpable.

Was it possible that Wang had already spilt the beans and told the MSS about the envelope?

Possibly. It was also possible that they didn't know anything and that it was a general question.

It didn't matter to Kryton. He was under strict instructions to assist the Chinese to find more intelligence – not to share it unnecessarily.

He just smiled at the two Chinese agents. The fact Yen didn't follow up with any leading or probing questions suggested to Kryton that they probably didn't know about the possibility of the SD card.

One of the younger analysts from the operations hub entered the small room, saying something to Agent Chen whilst gesturing to Kryton. Chen nodded as the analyst left the room and waited outside.

"You have a phone call," she said to him.

The Australian stood up from his seat and left the small room, following the analyst to one of the tables with numerous phones and equipment on it.

Chen and the Colonel stayed behind.

"Do you think he's telling the truth?" he asked her in Mandarin.

"I don't know. He's proven very reliable so far, if not a little reckless," she replied.

The Colonel nodded, sitting back down and continuing to prepare his debrief report.

The young analyst pointed to a phone on the side of the table. Kryton nodded to thank her, picking it up and placing it next to his ear.

The familiar voice of Jonas came across the line.

"Jesus. What is it about low profile that you don't understand?" he said, clearly aware of and not impressed that his operative had become caught up in a downtown car chase.

"Yeah, I'm fine, thanks mate. I appreciate you asking," replied Kryton firmly, not willing to take any beratement, especially after the day he had just had.

Jonas sighed.

"Yeah, fair enough. Are you okay?"

"I'll live," replied Kryton, gently looking down and rubbing his ribs. They had become numb.

"What's your update?" asked Jonas.

Kryton exhaled deeply.

"We've found the link between all the low-level operators and their boss. He's a special ops half-colonel who was tied in with some arms dealer. Apparently, this dealer was a big wig in their government until they booted him a while ago."

"Have the Chinese got them?" asked Jonas.

"Yeah. They're on their way to Beijing. The Chinese are going to give them a good go over."

"Okay. You're done there. Washington wants the focus back on Wallis. I'm bringing you back to Guam. A USAF plane is en route from Japan and should be there in a few hours."

Kryton looked over his shoulder at the office where Chen and Yen were both talking on their respective phones.

"That's good. Do you think they have any protein bars onboard? I haven't eaten in a while."

Jonas paused for a moment, thinking about the seemingly innocent question. Kryton could hear him mumbling away from the phone.

"Yeah, don't worry, you won't go hungry."

It seemed like a completely innocuous question. In reality, it was code used to tell Jonas that he had some important information, and that he wouldn't be able to share it over the Chinese phone, which they assumed would be bugged.

"Good. I'll see you in a few hours," said Kryton before hanging up the phone.

# 14

The Gulfstream aircraft effortlessly sailed through the pre-dawn sky at forty-five thousand feet. Kryton sat back in one of the passenger seats of the VIP transport plane, looking out into the darkness.

Not even the stars were out tonight.

He adjusted the ice pack that he held against his ribs, trying to reduce some of the swelling. He was used to the pain by now.

A young USAF airwoman, wearing a flight suit, came and tapped him on the shoulder.

"Sir, we've got the communications system up now," she said to him.

He nodded, getting up from his seat and moving to the rear of the plane, where a mobile encrypted video communications system had been set up so that he could talk to the SOCCE.

They had been in the air for three hours, but issues with the satellites had disrupted their ability to use the specialised system. He sat down and placed the set of headphones over his head.

He tapped the button on the laptop computer. The tired face of Jonas appeared on the screen.

"Geez, Jonas, have you slept lately?"

Jonas allowed himself a small laugh.

"No, not much. We've been trawling through everything the Chinese have sent us. It was a pretty decent collection of intelligence – for as much as they were prepared to give us, I'm sure."

"What did you find?" asked Kryton.

The highly encrypted system would allow them to have a Top-Secret level conversation.

Jonas scratched his head, looking down at some of his notes.

"Well, the guy called Wang has been on our scope before. He was on the ascendency in the CCP but had a falling out a few years back.

84

Apparently, he was more of a hardliner, and he thought some of the party changes were too moderate."

"He seemed to be having a good old time at the track. Certainly not the actions of someone who is anti-capitalist."

Jonas smiled.

"That's true, but it seems that after he was demoted, he turned to arms dealing, and became quite accustomed to the Western lifestyle."

"Or did he?" asked Kryton. "The Chinese have made the assessment that he funded the hiring of all of the low-level players in this. The Iranians, the PLA guys. They were trying to attack the meeting between Chinese and Taiwanese officials."

"You think he was just playing the long game?" asked Jonas.

"Sure. That's their culture. The attack on Air Force One and the attack in Taipei, if both had been successful – even if only one had been successful – would have almost certainly have caused a war. I think that was their aim. Nothing would have helped the hardliners *and* an arms dealer more than a war."

Jonas listened to Kryton's theory. It certainly made sense. The main conspirators on both sides had government connections. It was plausible that they were trying to initiate a regional war between the U.S. and China – and making it look like the other was responsible for starting it in the process.

"Okay. So, we'll let do the Chinese do what they will do with their traitors. What about on our side though? Where are we at with Wallis?"

"They've virtually closed Taiwan down looking for him. It should only be a matter of time."

"He can't be the only Westerner involved, though. There must be more people involved," said Kryton.

Jonas nodded in agreement.

"NSA is throwing all the data we've got through their systems. They're trying to see what other phones or communications are linked to both the tower on Zulu One, as well as the Hong Kong tower that the MSS used to identify Wang's probable location. CIA and ASIS are turning over every stone they can to try and get someone to talk. This is still the number one priority."

"What about the financial transactions. What did AUSTRAC find?"

"We're still looking at those. Money has been getting bounced all over the place, so we're sure we're on the right trail. Now that we know who has been involved, we should have some more fidelity soon."

Kryton leaned back into the plush leather seat of the plane. He had to stifle a yawn.

"When did you last sleep?" asked Jonas.

Kryton softly smiled.

"It's been a while. I don't even know what time zone I'm in."

Jonas nodded in empathy, stifling his own yawn.

"Oh, what else did you need to discuss? You used veiled speech on the phone back in Hong Kong."

"Oh shit," said Kryton, darting to sit upright in the seat.

He reached into the small pocket at the top of his jeans, pulling out the SD card he had retrieved from Jianwu. He held it up to the screen.

"I pulled this off of the guy I chased down in Honkers."

Jonas looked interested.

"Do the Chinese know we have it?"

Kryton shook his head.

"No. It was fun working with them and all, but I don't completely trust them. We can share with them whatever is on this later on if we want to."

"Good work. Get the airwoman to transfer the files back here. We can process it while you're in the air."

Kryton gave the thumbs up and smiled.

"Will do. See you in a few hours."

Jonas nodded his head before terminating the call.

Kryton stood up and walked to where the small team of signals analysts were sitting. He passed them the SD card, watching how they expertly electronically transferred the data files back to the SOCCE on Guam.

"Thanks," said Kryton in appreciation.

*It's all yours, Jonas,* he thought as he returned to his seat.

He pulled a water bottle from his bag, taking several sips as he looked out of the window, contemplating the next moves.

All he could think about was Wallis.

*Who was he?*

*Why was he involved?*

There was now no doubt that the conspiracy involved both Chinese and Western people – many who had significant access to classified resources. He took a moment to think about what could have been. How by sheer fluke a Timorese man witnessed a murder on a dark and rainy Dili evening. How fortunate it was that that man had links to an

86

intelligence operative who owed him a favour. What could have happened if so many things hadn't been the result of sheer luck.

Kryton couldn't help but laugh.

"Make sure you buy yourself a lotto ticket," he said to the face being reflected in the window by the dull internal cabin lights.

He closed his eyes, and in a few moments, was having some well-earned sleep.

# 15

The wind blew softly through the screen door of the farmer's small cottage. The wind chimes hanging on the porch slowly clanged in the breeze.

The owner of the cottage, a middle-aged bachelor, sat in the front living room watching the Major League Baseball on his television. He enjoyed the cool early autumn breeze wafting through the front door.

A dog started barking loudly out the front of the cottage, standing on the gravel driveway. The excited brown Labrador ran around in a circle, barking aimlessly into the night.

"Shut up," yelled the farmer from his recliner chair inside the cottage.

The dog continued its incessant barking.

The farmer sighed, placing his open can of beer down on the small table. He got up out of his chair, walked towards the front screen door, angrily knocked it open and walked out onto the porch.

"What the hell are you barking at?" he yelled at the dog.

The Labrador started growling. The farmer walked down the steps of the porch and looked down at the dog.

"What is it?" he said, now calmly patting the dog on the head.

A large clanging noise came from an area to the farmer's right side. He darted his head, looking over at his standalone garage. He started to walk over, cautiously approaching the front of the garage, his timid dog trailing several steps behind.

He walked to the front, opening up the large white wooden door slightly and stepping inside. He reached up to the side wall, flicking a switch that turned on the single globe that emanated a dull glow throughout the dusty interior.

The farmer stopped and looked around. In the centre of the garage was a dark blue single cabin pickup truck.

"Hello?" he said loudly.

He walked down towards the back, between the side of the garage and the truck. He gently approached the rear of the pickup, leaning his head around the corner. He reached his hand out to his left side, towards the nearby workbench while still looking around the back of the truck.

He grasped at fresh air, not finding what he was looking for. The farmer turned his head, finding an empty workbench where his pick-axe handle usually sat.

The dog barked loudly. It was an alerting bark.

The farmer turned around quickly.

His eyes widened as the force of the thick wooden handle was cracked over the side of his face. He instantly fell to the ground, unconscious.

His assailant moved over the motionless farmer, prodding at him with the handle. Ensuring that he was out cold.

It was Wallis.

The dog continued to bark until Wallis turned and growled at it, raising the handle above his head in a threatening manner.

The dog turned and ran out of the garage, its tail between its legs.

Wallis grinned, leaning down to raid the farmer's pockets. He found a wallet containing some cash and credit cards, a Zippo lighter, as well as the thing he was most hoping to find – a set of car keys.

Wallis moved the body of the still breathing farmer to the side of the garage before running to the larger doors and opening them, allowing enough room for the pickup truck to exit the garage. He opened the driver's side door, jumped in and looked around the cabin.

He turned on the ignition. The large six-cylinder truck came to life. Wallis gently drove it out of the garage, driving past the dog, which was now sheepishly lying on the porch, and off into the night.

# 16

The Gulfstream smoothly touched down on the runway at Anderson Air Force Base in Guam. The beautiful bright midday sky was scattered with fluffy white clouds. It reminded Kryton of many of the war movies made in the 1950's set in the islands of the Pacific Ocean.

The plane taxied to the apron, coming to a complete halt with a slight shudder. Kryton stood up, nodding to the small USAF contingent as he disembarked.

The bright sun caught him by surprise. He reached into his jacket pocket and pulled out his Oakley sunglasses, placing them over his eyes. He exhaled deeply. He never slept well on planes, but he had at least enjoyed a few hours of uninterrupted rest.

He walked off of the tarmac, recognising a familiar face standing by a Humvee near the terminal. Kryton walked up to the waiting man.

"G'day, Jonas," Kryton said, extending out his hand.

Jonas smiled, returning the handshake.

"How are you, mate?"

Kryton wasted no time, throwing his bag into the back of the large U.S. military vehicle.

"I've been busy," he said, looking at his friend and smiling.

He gingerly jumped into the passenger's side seat. His body was aching, the adrenalin of the past few days had worn off and it was now attempting to heal itself.

Jonas jumped behind the steering wheel, manoeuvring the Humvee off of the tarmac and onto a road that led to the old warehouse where the SOCCE was still located.

"We've got a doctor waiting back at the SOCCE, you'll get a full look over," Jonas said.

Kryton leaned back into the seat, taking in a deep breath of fresh air.

"That would actually be pretty good."

He looked out over the runway. It seemed a lot quieter than when he had first arrived to plan and launch the mission onto Zulu One.

"Where are all the planes?" he asked Jonas.

"They've been redirected to other missions or sent back to Hawaii and the States. Once we were confident that the Chinese government weren't behind all this, Washington reduced the strategic posture very quickly."

Kryton nodded. He turned around and reached into the back of the Humvee, where an esky containing water was sitting. He pulled one out, opened the bottle and drank most of the cool liquid in one go.

"I must still be a bit thirsty," he said amusingly to Jonas.

He closed the bottle and placed it down by his feet. He enjoyed having the wind blow over his face as the open-air Humvee moved its way along the small road.

"I tell you what, I'll be happy when I don't have to fly for a while," he said casually.

Jonas turned his head, looking at Kryton in an awkward manner.

"Oh," he said reluctantly.

Kryton kept looking forward and gritted his teeth. He knew Jonas had something to tell him. Something that he probably wouldn't like.

"What?"

"Well. I have some good news and some bad news," said Jonas.

Kryton sighed.

*Well, can't be anything too serious, not after the week I'm having,* he thought.

"Okay, bad news first."

Jonas was trying not to laugh.

"Alright. The bad news is, we're wheels up in just over an hour. That C-17 we drove past is our ride. We've been directed to mainland U.S. to continue operations."

Kryton slowly and curiously turned to look at Jonas.

"Why?"

Jonas pulled up to the front of the warehouse, applying the handbrake and turning the ignition off.

"That, my boy, is the good news. We've found Wallis."

Kryton suddenly pepped up. His eyes widened.

"Where?"

Jonas proceeded to jump out of the Humvee.

91

"Come inside, I'll show you. We have to move quickly, though, there isn't much time."

Kryton eagerly followed Jonas into the SOCCE. It was a hive of activity. Analysts were busily packing up cases with a myriad of equipment, ready to load onto various modes of transport. Everything from communications equipment to computers, weapons and television screens used to display information. All of it had to be accounted for.

"Where's my team? How's Cav?" asked Kryton.

"The Americans have already been pushed back to the States. Cav is back in Sydney getting his medical treatment. He's okay. He'll be offline for a week or two, though."

Kryton nodded his head as he looked around the room.

"Over here," said Jonas, gesturing to the small planning area where the mission onto Zulu One had been prepared from.

Kryton followed him to where a pair of young analysts were hovering over a laptop. The two young females wore the standard deployed analyst clothing – beige pants, a tight blouse and hiking shoes, with their hair tied back into a ponytail.

"This is Louise representing the Americans, and this is Olivia, she's one of ours," said Jonas, making his way around the table and standing over several maps and images.

"They're both intelligence analysts with experience at various agencies, and I've got them conducting the fusion of everything that's been coming in, which is all going back to Canberra and Washington," he added.

Kryton introduced himself to both of the young women. He noticed how tired they looked. He had to remind himself to remember that while he was in Asia chasing bad guys, there had still been a team back here in Guam working around the clock to support it all.

"Okay, Olivia. Why don't you give Mister Kryton a rundown on what we know."

The young analyst nodded dutifully.

"Sir, a little over an hour ago we received CCTV footage of a pickup truck entering a service station near the Canadian and U.S. border."

She tapped a button on the laptop and a black and white video from inside a well-stocked service station began playing, projected onto a whiteboard being used as a display screen. The four stood looking at the footage, watching as a man entered the service station. The man looked at several items on a magazine rack for a few minutes, then proceeded to the refrigerators. A moment later, he was paying for a couple of maps and two bottles of water.

"Can we get a better picture of this, another angle perhaps?" asked Kryton.

Olivia played with the buttons. There were now three videos playing simultaneously on the screen. One of them showed the CCTV from behind the counter, showing the customer paying for the drinks and maps.

"That's Wallis alright," said Kryton. "Where is this and when is it from?"

"It's about three hours old. A local farmer contacted the Canadian police saying that he had been attacked at his farm and his pickup truck stolen. That truck is this one here," said Jonas, pointing to one of the images with the pickup truck sitting by a fuel bowser.

"This is just outside of Toronto," added Jonas.

Kryton stood up from his leaning position. The look of surprise on his face was obvious.

"How the hell is he in Toronto?" asked Kryton in disbelief.

Jonas looked back at Olivia.

"Continue," he said to her.

"The Chinese shared their intelligence relating to the man you had the encounter with in Kowloon Bay."

"The special forces guy?" asked Kryton.

"Ahh, no. This guy," continued Olivia as she opened up an image of Jieng Wang onto the screen.

"Oh. Yeah, they told me about him. A former Communist Party official or something," said Kryton.

"A bit more than something," said Jonas. "He was in our databases, as well as the American ones. He was on his way up within the CCP before falling out with some of the moderates. He then made a fortune in dealing arms."

"How is he linked to Wallis, though?" asked Kryton.

"Well, that's how he was able to get into Canada. A black flight was tracked by NORAD entering Canadian airspace, occasionally popping on and off their radar."

"And?" asked Kryton.

"The plane was tracked to a remote airfield outside Toronto, where a random group of plane spotters noticed it, photographed it, and placed it on social media."

"People do that?" asked Kryton.

"Yes, sir," replied Louise.

"Why did this plane grab their attention?"

Olivia again tapped a button, displaying a picture of a corporate Lear jet, similar in shape and size to the Gulfstream that had returned Kryton to Guam.

"VIP jets don't often make appearances at tiny airfields used by crop-dusting planes. This one got noticed by the plane spotters. They spend all day just watching planes come and go," said the young Australian analyst.

Kryton looked at Jonas and could only chuckle.

"Each to their own," he said.

Olivia continued briefing.

"The numbers on the tail of the plane are registered to Wang Industries in Hong Kong. The plane belongs to Jieng Wang."

"The analysts at NORAD put out an alert on the flight, which was picked up by the analysts here, who matched it to the social media information," said Jonas.

Kryton tapped his fingers on his chin.

"So, Wang helped Wallis get back into North America?"

"We assess that's the case," said Louise.

Kryton took a step towards the screen, looking closely at the now still image of Wallis.

"But why? Why would a guy who is supposed to be a professional be so sloppy? Stealing a truck then going to a service station. Illegally flying into Canada. Surely, he knows that it can all be traced?" said Kryton, turning to look at the three of them.

Jonas looked at Olivia and nodded. She reached under the table and pulled out a leather satchel. She undid the clip and pulled out a red manila envelope. The marking 'Top Secret' was on the top of it.

"Oh, he knows," said Jonas. "He just doesn't care."

Kryton looked at Jonas curiously before he walked back to the table and took the small file Olivia handed to him. She continued explaining.

"We know that Wallis hired the Iranians to conduct the attack on Air Force One in Dili. With the intelligence you obtained in Hong Kong, and from what the Chinese have shared with us, we know that it was all funded by Wang, the arms dealer."

Kryton nodded as she spoke.

"We know that a small element of PLA special forces soldiers supported the logistics of the attack on Air Force One, and then also attempted to attack the clandestine Taiwanese and Chinese government meeting in Taipei. They were recruited by Wang."

"Okay. So, what else?" asked Kryton.

Jonas continued.

"But, what is the link between Wallis and Wang? Apart from the use of his plane, how did they end up being connected?" said Jonas.

"I don't know. Through financial arrangements, perhaps?" suggested Kryton.

Jonas took the file out of Kryton's hand and placed it down on the table, skipping a few pages and showing Kryton a summary page.

"This is everything that we managed to pull off of the SD card you transferred from the USAF plane on your way here. You know how you said that someone must have betrayed Wallis, by telling the Chinese about the location of Zulu One?"

Kryton nodded.

"The fact is that the same person must have told them about Wang and his special forces officer friend. This file was heavily encrypted, and we're still trying to decipher some of it. However, it has details of the financial exchanges between Wang and Wallis, but also has some cryptic details of someone who connects the two of them together. Someone at the top of the network."

"And someone big," added Louise, gesturing for Kryton to join her next to one of the whiteboards.

On it was a series of pictures, forming a pyramid from top to bottom. The sort of diagram seen in crime movies where the criminal network and its linkages are laid out. Kryton looked over it. It had all the familiar faces – Wang, Wallis, Jianwu. Below them were images of all of the lower level players, including at the bottom a picture of the Iranian man Behrouz, who Kryton had run into back in Dili.

At the top of the diagram was an empty box. Kryton leaned forward to look at the word written inside it.

"Phoenix," he whispered.

He turned around to look at the analysts.

"Who is Phoenix?"

"That's what we don't know. That name is in this file. Both Wallis and Wang have their link to each other through whoever Phoenix is. We think it's a codeword. Whoever it is must be big because very few people had information about both the meeting in Taipei *as well* as the location of Zulu One."

"How few?" asked Kryton.

Jonas scratched his head.

"Low double digits, if that," he said.

Kryton sat down for a moment, trying to comprehend it all.

It was one thing for a rogue NSA agent to go off of the grid, but now someone in the upper echelons was involved, too.

"It's not everything that's actually on there. We're still trying to unlock it all," said Jonas.

Kryton thought about the SD card for a moment, and what its purpose was. He then smiled.

"This is an insurance policy, isn't it!" he said to Jonas.

Jonas nodded.

"We think so. Once they knew they were betrayed, Wang compiled all of his knowledge about everything, placed in onto the SD card, and was offloading it to Jianwu when the MSS intervened. We think they were likely going to bargain with the U.S. to get asylum in return for exposing whoever Phoenix is. Phoenix had probably hoped that the MSS would have captured them all before they had the chance to do so."

Kryton sat down on one of the fold-away chairs and ran his hands through his hair. All of the pieces were slowly coming together, but unfortunately, there was still a serious player running around unchecked, and they still had no idea who it was.

"They must have encrypted the SD card in a manner in which they thought they would be the only ones who could unlock it. That was their bargaining chip," said Kryton.

"Most likely," said Jonas.

"But we still don't know one other key question. Do you know what that is?" Kryton said, looking at the two young analysts, the instructor in him always seeking an opportunity to pass on his skills and knowledge.

The two girls thought for a moment, until Olivia's eyes widened in a moment of inspiration. A small grin indicated she knew the answer.

"We don't know *why*," she said.

"Exactly!" Kryton said, clicking his fingers and pointing his hand at her in approval. "We don't know why. If we knew why, we might be able to work out their next step, which might help narrow down who Phoenix is. Let's come back to that later. You said Wallis doesn't care about being cautious. Why is that? Where is he now?"

Jonas looked at the two girls and indicated they should leave. The operation was in a very sensitive stage, and it was being conducted on an extreme 'need-to-know' basis. Once the analysts had politely departed, he turned to look at Kryton.

"Wallis crossed the border into the U.S. about an hour ago, and has now disappeared," said Jonas.

Kryton looked up at him, confused and shocked.

"Are you fucking kidding me?"

"Yeah, it was a bit of a screw-up. U.S. Customs has CCTV footage of the stolen truck crossing the border. He used a passport that had the same name as his own, but a different document number. It went unnoticed. The problem was, we've been looking for him internationally. The domestic agencies hadn't made it a priority."

"They should still have been on the lookout for possible fake I.D.'s," said Kryton.

"True. But what's done is done. The focus was in Asia. No one expected him to so brazenly sneak back into the U.S."

Kryton rolled his eyes. He couldn't help but laugh. Despite all of the cutting-edge technology they had available, nothing could fix the small cracks in the system that would allow someone to escape detection – such as human error.

"Okay, so what's his purpose now?"

"Well, the fact is you're right, his tradecraft has been sloppy. But I don't think he's trying to hide. I think he's on a revenge mission. He's after whoever betrayed him, and he knows exactly who it was."

Kryton sighed as he looked over the file. The parts that were actually deciphered showed a massive conspiracy, linking all the PLA members, Wallis, and all of the men Wallis had recruited, to a single point of connection – Phoenix. The financial funding details were also in there.

"Where is he going then?"

Jonas turned the laptop towards himself and tapped a few buttons. He found what he was looking for, turning the screen back in Kryton's direction. Kryton leaned over the table to get a better look at the display. It was a headline from the online version of the *Washington Post*.

'U.N. Security Council to meet Tuesday' it said in bold lettering across the top of the screen.

"You think he's going to New York?" asked Kryton.

"Yes, I do, but that's just my theory. The Mounties in Canada spoke to the service station attendant where Wallis stopped near Toronto.

Wallis was asking about the best routes for getting to New York State, and he bought a map too. He crossed into the U.S. near Niagara Falls."

Kryton looked at the screen. He shook his head slowly.

"Why would he go there, though?"

"As I said, only a handful of people had enough information to have been able to alert the Chinese, and this file indicates that that person was working with Wallis and Wang. Unless we can decipher it, we need another way to find out who Phoenix is."

"Can't we give the NSA more time to work over it?"

Jonas shook his head.

"Their initial checks indicate that it's heavily encrypted, and parts of the file had some sort of self-destruct feature that meant it was slowly erasing itself. Wang and Jianwu had set themselves up a pretty solid insurance policy."

"What's our plan?" Kryton asked Jonas.

The President and the CIA Director are aware of the leak, and now you can consider yourself aware of it too. We're part of only a very few people who are aware. Canberra is now facilitating this operation on behalf of the CIA. This is now the most sensitive counter-intelligence operation in the world."

Kryton placed his hands on his hips and tilted his head slightly. He had worked on some highly classified and sensitive operations in the past, but this was at a whole new level.

"The CIA Director has authorised us to chase this theory. We'll travel to New York and work with the Secret Service. They're enacting a massive operation to provide double protection around the U.S. officials who were privy to the details that were able to compromise Wang and Wallis. Some are still in Washington; the others are attending the U.N. in New York."

"What do the Secret Service think?" asked Kryton.

"They've been told about a threat to U.S. dignitaries coming from Wallis. All local law enforcement and federal agencies have a BOLO on him," said Jonas, referring to the 'Be On the Look Out for' information file that was often distributed to law enforcement agencies to help find a wanted person.

"However," he continued, "our *actual* task is to identify whoever Wallis tries to target. He might just lead us to Phoenix."

"Why don't we just detain Wallis and ask him who Phoenix is? They can grant him a reduced sentence or something," suggested Kryton.

"Certainly, that's an option, but have a look at the list of those who might be involved," said Jonas as he passed Kryton a sheet of paper.

Kryton couldn't believe the names on the list in front of him.

"This goes all the way up to —"

"That's right," said Jonas, cutting him off. "You think those people haven't got the ability to cover their arses!? No, we need to get intelligence that directly links the two of them together. If we can determine who it is, then we can chase that person down covertly and expose their involvement."

Kryton nodded as he folded the piece of paper up and handed it to Jonas.

"So, we're off to New York then."

It was a risky move based solely on a theory Jonas had. Wallis had proven himself to be a highly competent operator. He was now on home turf, where he might have a myriad of people with resources willing to help him. To perhaps even continue the original mission of assassinating the U.S. President. Then again, they might be wasting their time chasing ghosts.

"You've got thirty minutes. Clean yourself up, change your clothes and we'll head back to the airfield."

Kryton looked around the warehouse, which was now nearly empty. The mobile SOCCE would soon be fully packed up and off to its next destination.

New York City.

# 17

*Fort Hamilton Army Garrison*
*Brooklyn – New York*
0800 local – Tuesday

Kryton stood by a fence overlooking Gravesend Bay at the Fort Hamilton Army Garrison in the New York borough of Brooklyn. He turned to his right, looking up at the massive Narrows Bridge which linked the borough to Staten Island. The morning traffic was busily making its way along the foreshore.

The morning sun reflected off of the water, but a cold chill still permeated through the fresh autumn morning – or *fall* in the American parlance. The trees on the quiet military base were already turning a shade of brown and beige, and would soon be on the ground awaiting the chill of winter.

"Final brief's in ten minutes," came a voice from next to him.

Jonas handed Kryton a covert radio set.

"Seems like I've spent the last month listening to a voice in my head. The psychs will think I'm going crazy," said Kryton humorously.

Jonas chuckled.

Both men wore dark denim jeans, a polo top and a neat sports coat. The coats would keep them warm, but its main purpose was to conceal the pistols holstered to their belts.

"You'll need these, too. The Secret Service provided them, they'll allow us access to anywhere," said Jonas, passing Kryton an I.D. card with the U.N. logo on it, as well as the bald eagle of the U.S. Government.

They turned and walked back to the disused single-story building on the edge of the garrison, where they had established the mobile SOCCE.

"Are you up for this? It's been a while since you were in the field," Kryton asked Jonas.

"It had been a while since you had been in the field, but we gave you another go, didn't we!?" replied Jonas bluntly.

Kryton could only smile.

*Touché, good sir,* he thought to himself.

The men walked into the building. A small group of similarly dressed operators was sitting in a small huddle, facing a screen with an image of New York on it. It was overlayed with several pieces of data, mostly outlining the routes and timings of the key dignitary movements into the U.N. building positioned directly next to the East River.

A middle-aged male CIA field agent began the brief.

"Good morning. Today's operation is a target identification operation, aimed at locating the whereabouts of this person of interest, Peter Wallis," said the agent, pointing to an image of Wallis on the screen.

"This will be a joint DOD/CIA operation. We will be linked into the Secret Service as well as local law enforcement and federal agencies who will also be on the lookout for the POI whilst they provide protection for the U.N. Security Council meeting today in Manhattan."

The audience listened intently as the agent went through the brief.

Kryton was impressed with the thoroughness of it, covering everything from communications, actions to be undertaken on the sighting of the POI, right up to if there was a kinetic contact. It had been planned at very short notice, and much of it had been done during the sixteen-hour flight directly from Guam.

That was how intelligence needed to work. To be adaptable and expeditious.

"Additionally," added the agent, "our Australian counterparts are still embedded. They have full legal authority to conduct operations with us."

Kryton nodded and gave a small wave at the several curious agents, who hadn't seen him at Guam, who turned to look at the Australian operator.

The agent concluded the brief in a little under thirty minutes.

The agents would be divided into teams of two, conducting mobile patrols around the area, both on foot and in SUVs. The agent briefed that the intent was to intercept Wallis. Unknown to them was the covert task assigned to Kryton and Jonas to attempt to identify Wallis's likely target. To achieve that, they would be positioned closest to where the key dignitaries would be located.

A sound plan – but sound plans rarely survive the first contact.

"I heard you had a win at the races," said an American accent from behind Kryton.

101

He looked over his shoulder from his seated position.

"Hey, boys. How you going?" he said, shaking hands with SEAL operator Matt James, and CIA operator Rob Fox, both who had been in the thick of it with him during the mission to Zulu One.

"We're good. Glad to be back working with you today," said James.

"Me too. We'll get another crack at this little prick," said Kryton.

Both of the Americans laughed.

"If you get to him first, can you let me have a crack at him?" asked Fox, half-jokingly yet half-seriously.

Kryton could understand. Fox had been by his side when the Chinese naval artillery had almost blown them to the moon, and it was understandable that they blamed Wallis for that, along with the fact that he was a traitor. He'd love to have been able to tell the two Americans that it was, in fact, another American that had been responsible. Unfortunately, they still had to determine exactly who that was.

"No promises," replied Kryton simply, patting Fox on the shoulder.

"Step-off in five minutes," shouted the CIA agent across the room.

"See you lads for a beer tonight?" said Kryton.

The two Americans nodded, moving off to their SUV.

Kryton jumped into the passenger's side of his assigned SUV. Jonas took up his position behind the steering wheel.

"Have you got comms with Canberra?" asked Kryton.

Jonas pulled out a satellite phone.

"Secure comms back to a small ops team running things back home, and they will liaise directly to the CIA Director. She'll determine who gets briefed in from their end," he said.

"Cool," said Kryton, tapping on the dashboard and impatiently awaiting the order to depart.

"If Wallis is here, who do you think he'll be targeting?" asked Jonas.

Kryton sighed.

"No idea. The Chairman of the Joint Chiefs is going, so is the Secretary of State and the NSA Director. They're getting the Vice President to represent them at the Security Council, so it's a litany of highly ranked people. He must be crazy to have a go at any of them with the amount of security in place."

"I got a glimpse of his profile back on Guam. Highly trained and an ego the size of Texas. This guy probably thinks he can do anything," said Jonas.

Kryton nodded in agreement.

"You know, when I was lying on my arse in that stairwell in Taipei, he actually smiled before he was about to shoot me. Can you believe that!?" laughed Kryton.

Jonas laughed as well.

"That ego probably saved my life. It gave the Chinese girl enough time to scare him off," added Kryton.

He looked out the window and found himself exhaling deeply. It was the first time he'd taken a moment to appreciate just how close he had come to getting killed during all of this.

He thought for a moment about the task in front of them.

Even if Jonas was right, and Wallis was now turning on his own team and looking for revenge on whoever betrayed him, it didn't make a difference to Kryton.

He wanted both of them in a coffin.

# 18

Central Manhattan was abuzz. Most of the eastern side of Midtown had been closed off to road traffic by the NYPD, as well as Tudor City and Lennox Hill. Pedestrians used the opportunity to move freely, as locals continued their workday and tourists walked aimlessly with their heads in fold-out maps as they saw the various sights of the vibrant city.

Kryton and Jonas moved slowly through the city in their assigned SUV, easily passing through the police barricades with their I.D. cards. Helicopters buzzed overhead, keeping an aerial eye on the bustling city below and helping ensure that the massive security operation continued as smoothly as possible.

"This is crazy!" said Jonas, both of them having never seen such a mixture of law enforcement and federal security agencies in one place – not to mention all the undercover CIA, U.S. military and Secret Service agents mingling amongst the crowds.

"I suppose it can only help us," replied Kryton.

They drove along Second Avenue, parallel to the East River, listening in to all of the radio calls coming in from the various radio networks, all coming out through the speakers in the SUV. The analysts back in the SOCCE would be listening in to the same communications, and would discreetly guide the agents onto any targets of interest.

"Five hours and bugger all," mused Jonas.

Kryton turned his head to look at his friend.

"This is your theory. We could have stayed in Guam and got some fishing in," he said.

The other teams were scattered around the area. Several possible sightings of the POI had been reported but most were discarded as soon as they came in.

"We should make our way down to the U.N. building. The Council is wrapping up soon," said Jonas as they turned down East Fiftieth Street.

The two Australians drove towards the river, being careful to avoid the numerous pedestrians not watching where they were walking.

"All callsigns – this is One-Alpha. Stolen pickup truck identified in vicinity of the Brooklyn Navy Yard," came the voice from the SOCCE across their secure radio network.

"This is Dingo Seven – how long ago?" Jonas asked the SOCCE using the callsign for the Australian team.

"This is One-Alpha – we're currently checking all video footage from the area to gain fidelity on the POI. Wait, Out," came the reply.

Kryton turned his head to look at Jonas.

"He's here. I can feel it."

Jonas accelerated, honking at some pedestrians to move out of the way. They replied to him in typical New Yorker fashion – a polite extension of their middle finger.

He drove up a small back street and parked to the side near the gutter behind a row of police cars. The two operators adjusted their radios, ensuring they were ready for foot surveillance. They conducted another cursory check of their weapons.

Kryton felt a small surge of adrenalin. He smiled at Jonas.

"Looks like you might be right, mate," he said.

Jonas returned the smile and nodded. He too felt a sense of anticipation. They quickly but quietly started walking towards the U.N. building. Kryton pulled a small notebook from his coat pocket. He looked at the scribble of notes he had written down back at the SOCCE during the brief.

"All the U.S. officials are inside at the meeting, but it's about to wrap up. The Vice President is giving the main speech."

"Where are they going to after that?" asked Jonas as they quickly moved across the street and into a bricked pedestrian mall near East Forty-Seventh Street.

Jonas spoke into the radio and asked for more detail about the itinerary of the VIPs. The analysts checked their information, replying that the Vice President was due to host a meeting with some allied leaders after the speech, across the road from the U.N.

"Shit," said Kryton, looking around at all the of tall skyscrapers. "You could put a sniper anywhere here, not to mention being able to hide amongst all of the people."

"One-Alpha – how are they moving the VIPs across the road?" asked Jonas.

"This is One-Alpha – be advised that the Secret Service will be moving them across the road on foot."

Kryton looked at Jonas, bemused.

"She's going to use them as bait," he said.

"Fuck," Jonas whispered, placing his hands behind his head. "I knew she was appointed as CIA Director with a hard-arse reputation, but that seems cold."

"Maybe she trusts us to get the job done?" suggested Kryton.

Jonas glared at Kryton, a complete lack of confidence in their own ability written all over his face.

Kryton just laughed.

"C'mon," he said, "let's get closer."

Five minutes later, the two operators were standing next to The Isiah Wall, across the road from the U.N. building. Pedestrians were freely walking along the footpath, some even gathering near the barricades erected out the front of the U.N.

People were holding up all sorts of signs – seeking everything from world peace to the end of oil drilling in Texas.

Suddenly, the radio sprang to life.

"All callsigns – this is One-Alpha. Possible POI sighted moving north-east on First Avenue. Confidence is mild."

They looked at each other.

"Actual eyes on?" Jonas asked Kryton.

Kryton shook his head, looking up the street.

"Doubt it, I'd say they're tracking on CCTV."

He looked to his left. The Secret Service convoy was lined up on the side of the road in front of the building. Activity was starting to occur.

"They'll be coming out soon," said Jonas.

The radio spoke yet again.

"Sierra One – move to interdict possible POI between First and East Thirty-Fourth. Confidence is high."

"That's Fox and James," said Kryton.

Jonas nodded.

"He's heading towards here," he said.

106

"Split. I'll cover the other side," said Kryton as he proceeded to walk at pace to the other side of the road.

Kryton was starting to get that tingly feeling that all soldiers get when they expect to go into action. He took the map out of his back pocket, standing by the corner of the road and trying to look less conspicuous.

The pedestrian traffic was getting heavier. All that he had to go on was a face. One that was heavily imprinted in his mind.

"We need more info. Send a description," he said into his radio.

James's voice came across the network.

"I have POI in sight. Grey business coat and pants over a white collared shirt. Black leather shoes. Direction is north-east on First."

Kryton looked across the road and could see Jonas, looking up the street, also with a map out and pretending to be a tourist.

A moment later, James spoke again.

"POI now past East Thirty-Eighth. Still north-east on First."

Kryton shifted his position slightly so he was blocked from view by a small group of Chinese tourists who were standing around, waiting for their tour guide to come back. He could see up the street from where he was. If James was accurate, Wallis was now coming in their direction, and would be less than three-hundred metres away.

Kryton looked over his shoulder. The crowd seemed to have doubled in size as they waited for the U.S. delegation to depart the building.

"We're going to have to be up his arse," radioed Kryton.

"Let me take it, he knows what you look like," replied Jonas.

Kryton looked across the street. He could see Jonas, tucked up next to a family sitting on a bench and laughing. Jonas looked back at him, giving a subtle nod.

"POI is now past East Thirty-Seventh, same direction," radioed James.

Jonas looked intensely down the street, looking for a lone figure wearing a grey business suit. There were still too many people to get a firm visual.

"One-Alpha – do you have aerial sighting?" Jonas asked the SOCCE.

Back at Fort Hamilton, the analysts had already vectored a helicopter to the area. The pilot hovered high in the air on the other side of the East River. Its powerful camera telescope honed in on the direction of Wallis.

The analysts remotely enhanced the camera onto a lone figure walking up First Avenue.

"All callsigns – this is One-Alpha. POI is moving on foot north-east on First. Confidence is very high. Be advised we are preparing to interdict."

Kryton looked across the road at Jonas, who looked back at him.

"Now," mouthed Kryton to his friend.

Jonas nodded.

He turned his head slightly and discreetly covered his mouth with his map.

"One-Alpha – this is Dingo Seven. I am hereby taking operational control. Authorisation code is Lima; Mike; Three; Niner; Seven. Acknowledge please, One-Alpha."

Back at the SOCCE, the operations manager had a confused look on his face. He looked down at his assistant.

"Shit. Get Langley. Verify that code."

The assistant picked up the handset of a secure phone, instantly connecting to the operations room at CIA Headquarters in Virginia. A moment later, she placed the handset down and looked back at her supervisor.

"It's a valid authorisation code. Operational command is passed to Dingo Seven," she said.

"By whose authority?" he asked her.

"Director Dawn," she said simply.

The operations manager could only look back at his assistant, his mouth agape. She just shrugged her shoulders and turned back to face her workstation.

Jonas and Kryton covertly turned on their second communications channel. It would allow them to talk to each other without the rest of the world hearing. They would still be able to listen in to the calls from the other callsigns, and switch back to talk to them as necessary.

"I don't fucking like this, Jonas," said Kryton bluntly on their private channel. "Too many bloody people. We'll have a second to stop him attacking someone, *if* we're lucky."

The two men stood firmly in position, trying to get their own visual sighting of Wallis.

"Steady, mate. That's what we're here to do," replied Jonas.

"POI is same direction, now past East Fortieth," said One-Alpha, relaying the images from the helicopter.

"Got him? He'll be in our pockets in a minute," said Kryton.

Jonas sat down on the bench next to the family. He was worried that he would look too obvious just standing and looking up the road. He pulled his mobile phone out of his pocket and pretended to have a conversation, mumbling a few words every few seconds to fool any onlookers. His eyes focused intently up the street.

He momentarily caught a glimpse of something, which quickly disappeared behind a cyclist pushing his bike along the footpath. The footpath was very narrow, and the pedestrians were jockeying for a position because that part of the road had been closed off to all traffic, and was littered with various cars from the media and the law enforcement agencies.

Jonas tilted his head again, leaning his head forward slightly. He exhaled deeply. He lowered his head and pretended to scratch his nose.

"Got him. Inbound my direction, about fifty metres," he said to Kryton.

Kryton's head darted to the area as indicated by Jonas. It took him a moment, but soon he also had eyes on Wallis, who was casually walking up the street.

*Hello again, dickhead*, Kryton thought to himself.

He watched as Wallis continued walking up the street towards the U.N. building. Less than a minute later, the former NSA agent walked straight past where Jonas was sitting. Kryton waited a few seconds.

"Go now," he said.

Jonas stood up and casually turned to walk after Wallis. Kryton could see the two men from his position across the street. He slowly walked parallel to them, now approaching the front of the U.N. building. He looked ahead. The Secret Service and the NYPD had now blocked off the road, and an improvised walkway had been set up for the dignitaries.

"They're about to come out," Kryton said.

Jonas started walking quicker, trying to get closer to Wallis. The crowd was now lining the edge of the barricade, an even mixture of protesters and supporters, all loudly making noise.

"You'll have to stick to him like glue," said Kryton.

He could see Wallis across the road, less than twenty metres from him. Wallis moved to the rear of the crowd, easing his way towards the front by softly pushing people aside.

The crowd jockeyed for position, erupting in noise as the delegation departed the building and started walking towards the gated entrance. Jonas tried to get closer but was getting bumped amongst the crowd.

"Mate, if I get any closer, I'll be up his bum," he said to Kryton.

Kryton started walking across the street towards the crowd. He switched the button on his radio.

"One-Alpha – do you have eyes on target?"

"Negative. Target is obstructed by buildings and crowd," came the reply.

Kryton noted the condescending voice. It was as if they were saying: 'What did you expect would happen by pulling the other teams away?'

"Fuck this," murmured Kryton.

He made his way to the back of the crowd, intently looking through the sea of people to the direction where Wallis was last seen.

The crowd noise became even louder as the delegation walked through the main gates of the building and onto the street. The Vice President waved to a group of children, accompanied by a myriad of staff and Secret Service agents. The Chairman of the Joint Chiefs, as well as the NSA Director, both in full dress uniform, were there too.

Kryton moved his eyes like a hawk seeking its prey. He knew he would have to get to the front of the barricade, as that's where Wallis would likely be if he was going to try anything.

"Excuse me…pardon me," he said as he gently moved people aside.

"Visual?" he asked Jonas.

"Negative. Shit, it's like a bloody football match here," replied Jonas.

Kryton could see that the Vice President was now walking along the front of the barricade, shaking hands with enthusiastic members of the crowd, some even waving small American flags. The two military officers were standing a few feet behind him, next to some other officials.

A large woman turned to move away, creating a space in the throng. Kryton was now looking over the heads of a group of school children. Their diminutive stature ensured that Kryton could clearly see the suited man standing about six or seven metres in front of him, facing slightly away.

Kryton's eyes narrowed as he looked down the barricade towards Wallis. The dignitaries were about fifteen metres away behind his right shoulder. He moved his hand down to his holster, placing his hand over his pistol.

"Jonas, I have him," he whispered into the radio.

"Say again," replied Jonas, barely able to hear the voice in his ear over all of the noise.

Kryton watched as Wallis slightly turned towards the front. He could see something in his left hand, but he wasn't sure what it was.

*Fuck this*, he thought to himself, not prepared to allow a political assassination to occur that could also result in innocents being killed.

"I'm interdicting," he said into the radio, knowing Jonas was also nearby and could hopefully assist.

"WALLIS," screamed Kryton, his pistol now by his side.

The American turned, looking straight at Kryton. The Australian could see a black item in the former NSA agent's hand. He shot his arms up, aiming at the American.

It wasn't a weapon that Wallis was holding, but rather a phone, placed against his ear.

Kryton could feel time almost come to a complete halt as Wallis looked straight back at him, instantly recognising him. The American smiled slightly, as if he was completely at ease. He whispered something into the phone before turning to look over his left shoulder and up to the several storied brick building across the street.

Kryton followed Wallis's eyes up to the windows in the building. All had curtains over them.

All except one. One with its window slightly ajar.

He squinted, trying desperately to see what was in there. He saw movement.

"GUN, GUN, GUN," he shouted at the top of his voice.

A lady screamed the moment she saw Kryton's pistol by his side. This caused several of the school children to scream as well.

"Gun, go…go, go," screamed several of the Secret Service agents as instinct and training kicked in. They each began to initiate their well-rehearsed and tested drills as a shot rang out from up at the window where Wallis had been looking

Kryton quickly holstered his pistol, knowing full well that the reaction he was seeking from the Secret Service would include looking for threats. They would shoot first and ask questions later.

The crowd noise quickly turned from one of enthusiasm to one of sheer panic. Parents grabbed their children, desperately trying to get out of the area. People pushed and shoved as they tried to run away in any direction where there was clear space. The Secret Service had already bundled the Vice President into the convoy of armoured cars, whose tyres were now screeching on the road as they attempted to exfiltrate the scene up First Avenue.

NYPD and Secret Service agents, all with respective weapons drawn, looked aimlessly up and down and around the area, seeking to find the source of the shooting. Kryton turned to look back at Wallis, who was trying to get past an old man who was blocking his escape. Kryton was about to chase when he felt a massive thud in his back, driving him to the ground. The air in his lungs was knocked out, almost winding him.

An NYPD officer had identified the source of the warning and had run over to tackle Kryton, thinking he was the threat.

Kryton grimaced as he tried to turn his body. A second officer arrived at the spot; his pistol drawn straight at Kryton's head.

"Don't you move," shouted the young male officer.

"No. Get the fuck off… I'm with –" Kryton angrily attempted to say before the tackling officer drove a knee into Kryton's side, once again knocking the wind out of him.

"Secret Service…Secret Service," shouted Jonas as he arrived next to the officers, his hand raised showing the I.D. card provided to them earlier. The standing officer looked at it as Jonas also showed his pistol and radio.

"That was Peter Wallis, you have a BOLO on him. We need to go after him," he said to the officers.

The two policemen looked at each other, nodding in agreement. They both helped Kryton to his feet.

"That way," he said to Jonas, pointing to a footpath leading away from the river.

Kryton and Jonas sprinted up the narrow side street, seeking to locate the direction where Wallis had fled. Pedestrians were still running in all directions. The sound of police sirens echoed across the streets as several more helicopters started hovering over the scene.

"One-Alpha – we're in pursuit of POI, in vicinity of Second Avenue, we request support to intercept and capture," Kryton informed the SOCCE.

"Copy. Vectoring teams onto your position," replied the SOCCE.

The two Australians reached Second Avenue and looked up and down. The streets were still blocked off, but people were still moving about. A fire truck and ambulance raced past them, sirens and lights blaring.

"There!" said Jonas, pointing up towards the south.

Wallis was sprinting along the middle of the road. The two men gave chase. He had at least fifty metres on them. They continued chasing him.

"South past East Thirtieth…south past East Twenty-Ninth," they kept calling to the SOCCE as they raced past the street signs.

Wallis suddenly bolted to his right and up a narrow path between buildings. Jonas and Kryton followed.

The loud metallic thud of a bullet striking a large industrial bin met the two operators as they entered the narrow side street.

"Shit," exclaimed Jonas as he pushed Kryton out of the way.

Both men hugged the wall, drawing their own pistols and getting down onto their knees. They stuck their heads around, pistols raised and looking for the threat. They could see Wallis continuing to run away.

Once again, they chased, carefully moving up the side street and out on to Third Avenue.

"Shots fired. Now south on Third Avenue," said Kryton.

They continued to follow Wallis, transitioning from a sprint into a middle-distance stride. The helicopters started appearing overhead, vectored onto the area by the SOCCE.

Wallis noticed this, moving off of the road and continuing to run along the footpath, where the awnings and rooves of the shops would afford him some cover.

He kept running. Past East Twenty-Sixth; past East Twenty-Fifth; still trying to evade his motivated pursuers.

Less than four minutes later, he hit East Twenty-Third Street, where the road traffic was now moving. He darted to his right, now running west.

Kryton and Jonas were gaining. The gap between them slowly closed. Forty metres. Thirty metres.

As Wallis got onto Park Avenue South, he was almost hit by a car. Its irate driver honked his horn. Wallis pushed himself off of the bonnet of the car, raising his weapon and forcing a yellow taxi to stop. He reefed the driver out, throwing him down onto the road before jumping behind the steering wheel and tearing off up the road, tyres screeching.

Kryton and Jonas crossed the road, watching as Wallis drove off.

"Get one," said Jonas, pointing to another taxi that had been forced to stop when Wallis hijacked the first taxi.

Kryton pulled his I.D. card out along with his pistol, showing both to the terrified driver behind the steering wheel.

Jonas opened the driver's door.

"Federal Agents. We need your car," he said to the driver.

The poor man willingly got out as Kryton jumped into the passenger's front seat. He quickly looked over his shoulder. A well-dressed Wall Street type was looking back at him, confused.

"Take the bus, mate," he said, holding his pistol up over the seat.

The man didn't have to be asked twice. He jumped out of the taxi, just as Jonas engaged the gearstick and drove off up the road in pursuit of Wallis.

The two taxis tore south along the road, weaving in and out of traffic. Kryton kept relaying locations to the SOCCE, hoping that another team might be able to intercept.

They continued south. Past Union Square Park. Through Noho and down into Little Italy. The driving was dangerous. Pedestrians dived for their lives as Wallis crossed the lines and onto the other side of the road in order to weave between the traffic.

"This is worse than Hong Kong," mumbled Kryton under his breath, tightly gripping the coat hanger handle on the internal taxi roof as Jonas skilfully continued the pursuit.

The two looked at each other in utter disbelief as they barely missed hitting a group of cyclists crossing the road. Both considered, if only for a moment, abandoning the chase.

Their doubts were quickly quashed as the SOCCE made contact.

"Dingo Seven – this is One-Alpha. The NSA Director has been shot, his condition is unknown at this time. You're authorised to use any means necessary to neutralise the target."

"Shit," said Kryton. "He must have been after the NSA Director."

Jonas yelled at people to move out of the way, honking the horn as he continued driving.

"I suppose that makes sense, for it to have been someone in the NSA," he said.

The *who* and the *why* didn't matter at the moment. They both knew what was meant by the term 'neutralise'. It simply meant to stop Wallis, using up to and including lethal force.

# 19

The speeding taxis continued south through the lower end of Manhattan. They were now on Lafayette Street – a single laned road bordered by tall buildings and the occasional public park.

Wallis flew across an intersection whilst the light was red, barely missing another passing taxi. Jonas cautiously passed through, honking the horn of the taxi, before once again flooring the accelerator as they crossed the intersection to the other side. They were quickly approaching the government end of the borough, where the mayor's office and the main law courts were located. The pedestrian and vehicle traffic in this area was particularly busy.

"He's got nowhere to go," said Kryton as their taxi inched closer to Wallis.

"It's a miracle we haven't hit anyone. Where the hell are the other teams?" he asked.

They both knew that in a dense city such as New York, it was hard to get anywhere fast.

Wallis could see his pursuers in his rear-view mirror. He kept speeding along, but was now slowly being obstructed by the increasing traffic. Kryton and Jonas were now only two car lengths behind.

As Wallis approached City Hall, he took his eyes off of the road at the worst possible moment. A hot dog cart vendor was pushing his cart across the road, seeking to get a better position for his sales. Wallis looked forward again, seeing the cart and a stationary van blocking any possible continual movement.

He pulled hard on the steering wheel whilst applying the brakes, forcing the rear of the taxi to kick out. The taxi had too much momentum and continued off the road and up onto the footpath.

It crashed with a loud bang into another food cart, sending its contents sprawling across the concrete. Several pedestrians were also knocked over. Wallis's taxi came to a rest next to a large tree. The impact snapped his neck forward, smashing his forehead on the dashboard.

The carnage forced several cars and trucks on the street to all come to a sudden halt. Jonas's eyes widened as he saw a wall of metal in front of him. He slammed the brakes, turning the steering wheel and trying to avoid the delivery truck less than a few metres in front of them.

The taxi mounted the footpath and crashed into a post box, knocking it over. The driver's side door was wedged against a street light, preventing Jonas from being able to get out. His face had taken the full brunt of the steering wheel, cutting open his upper lip. Blood poured into his mouth and down his chin.

"Go…go get him. I'll call it in," he said to Kryton painfully.

Kryton extracted himself from the taxi, aided by several pedestrians. He looked across the road to where the other taxi had ploughed into a food cart. He started running towards it, brushing off the people simply trying to provide assistance.

Wallis managed to get out of his taxi, nursing a cut above his head that was trickling blood down the side of his face. He turned his head and saw Kryton moving towards him. He tried to move through the bystanders, all standing around, many with mobile phones out and filming the carnage.

He pulled his pistol out and fired two shots into the air. That had the desired effect, forcing the crowd to part, allowing him an escape. He ran across the road, ascending a small incline on the footpath where people were walking along two divided lanes.

It was the start of the Brooklyn Bridge walkway.

Kryton chased, weaving between the crowd and the stationary traffic that had gathered around the crash scene.

"Move, move," he shouted as he slowly moved through the bustling hordes.

In a moment he too was also on the walkway, running again after Wallis. The walkway gradually ascended so that it was now in the centre of the bridge, running parallel to the road lanes several feet below it. The wooden beams of the walkway clattered as Kryton sprinted after Wallis.

"On Brooklyn Bridge on foot, crossing away from Manhattan," he said into his radio.

In less than three minutes, the two men were in the centre of the bridge. Wallis occasionally looked over his shoulder, and could see that Kryton was closing. As he made his way under one of the famous brick arches, he turned and pointed his pistol at Kryton.

Wallis fired two rounds at the Australian, now less than thirty metres away. Kryton instinctively turned his shoulder, deliberately standing in front of a young female tourist who was, unfortunately, standing next to him.

He braced for the impact.

There was none.

Wallis had missed, the bullets flying harmlessly over the railing and likely into the water below.

Kryton turned and continued the chase. He was now breathing heavily. The run was becoming a slog. He could hear a helicopter hovering to the right-hand side, quickly followed by another on the left.

"Aerial support over the bridge, we have visual of POI," came the voice from the SOCCE into his radio.

The presence of tangible support motivated Kryton. He knew that Wallis would now feel like a wild animal, slowly being circled by a pack of predators.

Wallis kept running, weaving between pedestrians and knocking over an elderly lady.

"Hey," shouted her husband as Kryton sped past them both, rapidly closing in.

Wallis was now on the other side of the bridge. The walkway started descending into the Brooklyn side, easing the pressure on his tired limbs. He soon found the walkway exit, dashing down the stairs and onto the street below. Kryton cautiously followed, his pistol raised and ready to engage Wallis should he be waiting in ambush.

He wasn't. Wallis had exited the stairs of the entrance and followed the footpath up the street. Kryton slowly chased, following the trail of annoyed pedestrians knocked out of the way by Wallis. In a moment he too was on the street. He was now in a small tunnel.

He looked left and right.

Nothing.

"Shit," he said to himself.

He looked left and saw two young backpackers, one helping his friend who was on the ground, nursing his arm. H rushed over to them.

"Where did he go?" he demanded, assuming one of them had been knocked over by Wallis.

The standing backpacker pointed up the street, back towards the river side.

Kryton raced to the corner and ran across the road towards an intersection now on the other side of the bridge. He looked up the street, seeing Wallis's grey suit running up the footpath.

Kryton quickly looked up at the street signs, trying to identify his location.

"I'm on Old Fulton Road, in pursuit towards the river," he said.

He could hear sirens not far from his location. He hoped it was the support he was after.

The noose was tightening, Wallis could feel it. Blood continued to stream down his face as his legs started to cramp up. He continued running, and in three-hundred metres he came to a dead-end near the river. He tried to cross the street but was knocked over by a police car that came screaming to a halt. Wallis was knocked onto his backside. He turned as the officer exited the car, trying to bring his weapon to bear onto the traitorous NSA agent.

Wallis raised his pistol, firing several shots into the car door, forcing the officer to run and dive behind the rear of his own car. Wallis jumped back onto his feet, running towards the river along a boardwalk.

Kryton came flying across the road, still in pursuit. The beautiful Manhattan skyline opened up in front of him as he passed the famous Ample Hills Creamery.

Wallis limped towards the river, bumping into people as his injuries started catching up with him, incapacitating his ability to move. The pedestrians could see the chase unfolding. Some scattered, others watched in morbid fascination. Several more NYPD vehicles arrived on the scene – lights and sirens blaring.

Kryton followed, slowing to a light jog as he came within twenty metres of Wallis. He raised his pistol directly at Wallis's head.

Wallis turned, seeing that Kryton was now almost on top of him. He lunged at a young female tourist, grabbing her around the neck in a chokehold and pointing the pistol at her head. The terrified girl whimpered as she struggled under Wallis's grip.

Kryton maintained his sight picture on Wallis. He noticed an NYPD officer nearby, his weapon also raised at Wallis.

"Back down – Secret Service," he barked at the officer.

The officer looked at Kryton, probably confused by his Australian accent. He did as he was told, though, having been informed of Kryton's characteristics by the SOCCE as they vectored the support towards the intelligence operator.

Wallis then pointed his pistol at Kryton, pushing his head as close to his hostage's as possible in order to reduce his profile. He was breathing heavily and struggling to stay on his feet.

"It's over, Peter," Kryton said to him, his own pistol still pointed at Wallis's head.

Wallis could hear all the sirens, as well as the two helicopters now hovering over the river. He turned to look at them, assessing his chances.

The fact was, they were zero.

He lowered his head, taking in deep breaths.

Kryton inched closer.

Wallis looked straight at Kryton.

"Who the fuck *are* you?" he said to the Australian.

Kryton just looked at him. He lowered his pistol to down by his side.

"I'm no one, mate," he replied.

Wallis looked around once again. He knew it was hopeless. He lowered his weapon and released the girl, pushing her away. She ran away towards the police officers, crying as she clutched her bag.

Kryton stood directly in front of Wallis, about fifteen metres away. He could see Wallis tapping his fingers on the trigger guard of his pistol, still breathing heavily. His mind was obviously racing.

"Put it down," Kryton said to him, his own pistol still by his side.

Wallis lowered his head slightly. His eyes narrowed. A small grin appeared on his face.

*Oh, shit*, thought Kryton.

"Don't you do it," he screamed at Wallis.

Wallis shot his arm out, his pistol now pointing at Kryton.

Kryton responded in kind. Years of instinctive shooting drills ensured he got the first shot off. He twisted his wrist and fired his pistol from next to his hip. The bullet hit Wallis in the leg, buckling him. Kryton quickly raised his arms, bringing his hands together and firing two well-aimed shots into Wallis's upper chest.

The grey-suited man fell backwards into a garden bed, his pistol falling onto the wooden beams of the boardwalk.

A woman screamed as a swarm of NYPD officers ran into Kryton's view.

"Paramedic support requested," said one into his radio.

Kryton lowered his weapon and applied the safety catch. He walked up next to Wallis, looking down at the hapless man, his crisp white shirt bloodied from his wounds.

Wallis looked back up at him. His breathing was laboured. Kryton kneeled down next to him. A trickle of blood came down from the corner of Wallis's mouth. He looked at Kryton, his eyes showing fear. Wallis raised his hand slightly towards Kryton and mumbled something.

Kryton looked at him, curiously.

The Australian reached down and took Wallis's hand, almost as a last sign of mutual respect between two professionals who had gone up against each other.

Wallis tried to mumble something again. Kryton leaned down, placing his ear next to Wallis's mouth.

Life was slowly draining from his body.

Kryton listened closely as Wallis whispered into his ear. He then leaned back, looking down as Wallis tilted his head to the side, struggling to breathe.

Kryton stood up as the paramedic team arrived, looking down on the bloodied body in front of them. He moved to allow them to work, even though he quietly thought it was futile.

He walked into the middle of the boardwalk. NYPD cars and officers had swarmed the area, clearing away the terrified civilians and setting up a crime scene.

"Jonas," he said into his radio, "come and get me."

# 20

Kryton sat alone in a comfortable blue leather chair in a small room in the West Wing. He tapped his fingers on the wooden armrest. He tilted his head, slightly adjusting his necktie which was far too tight. He looked up at the wall, observing a beautiful oil painting depicting General George Washington crossing the Delaware River in choppy conditions.

*I'll bet you were standing up in those conditions*, Kryton thought to himself sarcastically, amused at his own humour.

He leaned forward, looking at the magazines and newspapers spread neatly on the table before him. He noticed the current edition of the *Washington Post*.

The lead article was still talking about the visit of the Australian Prime Minister to Washington, and how the relationship between the two countries was critical for dealing with potential conflicts in the South China Sea.

He read a few paragraphs. Even though the Security Council meeting had been an effort to promote peaceful relations in the region, and where the Vice President had publicly announced that China was not responsible for the attack on Air Force One, there was already a push from some 'vocal patriots', as the newspaper was quoting it, within Congress for greater military presence in the region to ward off a growing China.

Kryton just shook his head and smiled. He was used to doing the bidding of political masters who often had no idea of what it was really like at the coalface of their decisions – and who often wouldn't listen even when actually told.

A small piece in the bottom corner talked about the incident in New York. It said that there was still no more information about the person killed during a shoot-out in broad daylight in Brooklyn. A man linked to the assassination attempt on the NSA Director.

He flipped the paper over, trying to see if any of the sports scores grabbed his interest.

The door to the entrance of the room opened. The President's secretary entered. Kryton stood up, fastening the button on his bespoke charcoal suit and smiling at her.

"The President will see you now," she said politely.

Kryton nodded, following her up a short hallway. He noticed how enclosed and quaint the White House actually was. More of a large house rather than a series of office spaces. He thought to himself that it might be a nice place to work. Something homely about it. Certainly not somewhere you'd expect that the leader of the free world might order a nuclear strike from.

They entered the secretary's office, walking between two desks and to the front of the Oval Office. The secretary knocked twice. Kryton followed her in.

"Mister President – Sergeant Zach Kryton," she said, announcing the Australian operator to the President of the United States.

Kryton looked over at two men sitting across from each other in cushioned sofa chairs, sharing a joke over a glass of whiskey, as if they were old acquaintances.

President Lang looked up.

"Yes, yes. Come on in," he said in a most friendly southern manner, standing up and waving Kryton over.

Kryton thanked the secretary as she left, then proceeded over to the President, shaking his outstretched hand.

"Nice to meet you, Mister President," he said confidently.

"Well it's a god-damn pleasure to meet you, son," said the President, slapping Kryton on the back.

Kryton had to try not to laugh. He'd been briefed by the secretary that the President was very friendly, but the joviality still caught him by surprise.

"Do you know Ed? He's one of you," said Lang, pointing down to Prime Minister Ed Kernahan.

The Australian Prime Minister stood up, shaking Kryton's hand.

"Welcome to Washington," said Kernahan.

"Drink?" asked Lang to Kryton, standing over the small drinks table adjacent to the Resolute desk.

122

"Umm," murmured Kryton, not expecting the offer and looking at the Prime Minister for some guidance.

"He's not going to accept a no, mate. You should have one," advised Kernahan, grinning and sitting back down to take a drink from his glass.

"Well…yes, sir. I'd be delighted," said Kryton.

The President poured a drink into a crystal glass and handed it to Kryton. He offered the Australian a seat, which Kryton took up next to his Prime Minister.

Lang sat down in a cushioned seat in front of his desk.

"Well, this country owes you a massive debt of gratitude. As do I, for that matter," said the President.

Kryton nodded, taking a nervous sip on his drink.

"Just doing my job, sir," he said to the President, instantly kicking himself for not having come up with a better response.

Lang laughed. The three men spent the next few minutes engaging in casual conversation, sharing a drink and discussing all that had happened.

The door from the other side of the room opened, the one leading to the President's Chief of Staff's office. CIA Director Anna Dawn walked in carrying a thick briefcase. She placed it down on the table.

The demeanour in the room changed, taking on a more serious tone.

She opened the case and pulled out a file. It was marked 'Top Secret'.

"Is this all of it?" asked the President, taking it off of her and looking over its contents.

"Yes, sir. A full decryption," replied Director Dawn, sitting down on one of the sofas, opposite Kryton and the Prime Minister.

They allowed the President to look over the documents for a few minutes.

"Fuck me," he audibly whispered.

Lang exhaled deeply, closing the file and placing it on the coffee table in front of him. He stood up, looking at Dawn as he walked over to his desk.

"Are you ready for this?" he asked her.

"Yes, Mister President. Umm, sir, maybe our friends should –"

"No. They get to stay," he said, cutting her off.

The President pressed the button on his intercom, leaning down to talk into it.

"Helen, send in the Vice President, please."

"Yes, sir," she replied over the intercom.

A few moments later, the same door that Kryton had earlier come through opened.

Vice President Kendrick entered. He looked surprised. It wasn't often that he was summoned without context.

"Matthew, have a seat," said the President curtly, pointing to the chair at the long end on the other side of the coffee table.

Kendrick looked down at the other people in the room, before unbuttoning his jacket and sitting down. He crossed his legs.

Kryton leaned back into the sofa.

"Mister Prime Minister, I particularly liked your remarks out in the Rose Garden earlier," said Kendrick, trying to ease the awkwardness he felt.

The four of them just looked at Kendrick.

The Vice President looked around, confused by the manner in which he was being looked at.

Kryton could understand why the Vice President was feeling that way. He had already been briefed in by the Director. The Vice President hadn't been called in for a polite conversation.

It was an ambush.

President Lang leaned forward in his seat, glaring straight at Kendrick.

"You couldn't have waited another four years to get my job, you stupid son of a bitch," barked Lang.

Kendrick uncrossed his legs. His mouth suddenly dried up. He looked confused, staring at the others in the room with his mouth agape. Kryton stared at the President's deputy, showing no emotion at all.

"Mister President, I have no idea what you're talking about," protested Kendrick.

"A coup. A coup against me you disloyal mother…"

The President cut himself off, standing up and walking over to his desk. Kryton could see the tall man clenching his fist. For a moment, he thought that he might actually throw something at the Vice President.

Kendrick turned in his seat, looking to the CIA Director for support.

"Anna, please. What is this all about?"

Dawn just looked at the Vice President for a moment. A look of disgust. She turned to look at the President, who was now leaning on his desk. He gained his composure. He nodded back at Dawn.

She leaned forward, opening the file.

"The intelligence communities of both the U.S. and Australia have been working around the clock to link all the connections behind this conspiracy," she said.

The Director laid out a diagram in front of the Vice President. He leaned in to have a look. Kryton could see from where he was sitting that it was the network diagram of all the players involved.

Wallis, Wang, Jianwu. All the way down to the Iranians hired by Wallis.

"This is everyone we know to be involved. All are either dead or in captivity. All except for the person in that empty space in the box at the top of the sheet you're holding," said Lang.

The Vice President looked at the diagram, then around the room.

"Mister President, perhaps you and I need to talk in private," said Kendrick.

"To be fair, Matthew, you never had a chance. From the moment my young Australian friend here miraculously stopped the attack on Air Force One, you were on the backfoot. The fact is, you never planned on failure – and you've been trying to cover your tracks ever since."

Kendrick still looked confused, trying to argue his innocence.

"This file in front of you, Mister Vice President, is a comprehensive list of all the financial and communications contact you've had with everyone on that diagram," said Dawn.

"It was obtained by Mister Kryton during his mission in Hong Kong. It seems Mister Wang didn't take too kindly to being betrayed," she said, placing down an old file picture of Wang and Kendrick at a dinner from several months back.

Kendrick looked down at the photo.

"So, I know him. So what?" said Kendrick.

"You insult our intelligence community, Matthew. They have been able to correlate every transaction listed on the file that Wang had put together of interaction with you. Your communications directing the attack, getting him to fund it, and, to organise like-minded Chinese military personnel to run it," said Lang. "They were going to give it to us to barter for their own safety."

Kendrick just shrugged his shoulders and sat back in his seat.

"You're going to take the word of some commie?" asked Kendrick.

"The Chinese were told about the location of the island where the attack was organised from, and they were also warned about the pending attack on their conference with the Taiwanese," continued Director Dawn.

"So?" said Kendrick arrogantly, trying to keep his composure.

"They assessed that whoever organised the failed Air Force One attack was trying to get rid of the people involved. So did we. Since everyone known to be involved in the attack was either in captivity or on the actual island, it had to have been leaked to them by someone else who knew and who was involved. Someone on our end with access to our intelligence. Therefore, we started intercepting the phones of the very few people who were privy to that information about the location of the island. One of them, Mister Vice President, was you."

"How dare you. I'm the Vice President of the United States, who you gave you the authority to –"

"I did, Matthew," interjected the President. "You got sloppy. You know, when Anna first brought this to my attention, I couldn't quite figure out the relationship between you and Peter Wallis. In fact, we may never have known, if it wasn't for the fact you had spoken to your nephew. Your conversations make for interesting listening,"

Director Dawn pulled a small portable tape player from out of the case, placed it on the table and pressed play.

The sound of two men talking began to play from the speakers.

One was clearly the Vice President.

They listened for about a minute.

The tape had the Vice President trying to reassure a young man, who is identified on the tape as his nephew. It had the Vice President telling the man, also an NSA agent, that since Wallis was dead, there were now no more linkages to them, and that all would be okay.

Dawn stopped the tape.

"That means nothing, it's a private conversation between me and my nephew. The boy worked for Wallis on an assignment. He was just upset that Wallis had been involved and was worried he might be implicated."

Lang looked over at Kryton.

"Tell him."

Kryton sat forward. He cleared his throat and interlocked his fingers.

"Sir, when I shot Wallis, he was on the ground. He was bleeding and clearly believed that he wasn't going to make it. He pulled me down and whispered into my ear,"

"And what did he say?" asked the Vice President condescendingly.

Kryton looked at the President, then back at Kendrick.

126

"He said that the Vice President was Phoenix."

Kendrick just smiled and raised his palms.

"That could be anyone, Jack."

The President simply ignored him and his disrespectful tone.

Instead, he sat back down on the seat and turned to the Director.

"Anna, what is the codename for the Vice President as exclusively used by the NSA?" he asked, already knowing the answer.

Dawn looked over at Kendrick.

"It's Phoenix, Mister President."

Kendrick stood up, shaking his head.

He desperately tried to regain the initiative.

"I don't know what wild stories you're getting told by these people, Jack. This file is a whole bunch of circumstantial evidence, at best. You've got some codename that I'm sure many people at the NSA have access to, and you're linking that to something supposedly said by a dead man, who whispered it to some...some no one?" he said, arrogantly pointing at Kryton.

The Vice President turned to walk out.

"*Is* he dead, though, Matthew?"

Kendrick stopped in his tracks. He turned his head and looked at Lang. The President had a look on his face that suggested that he had just snagged a royal flush in a poker tournament.

Director Dawn opened the case again and pulled out a small tablet. She tapped a few buttons, then proceeded to speak into it.

"Are you ready?"

A voice replied from the other end.

"Yes, Madam Director."

She nodded, turning the screen towards where the Vice President had been sitting. Kendrick slowly sat down, looking at the screen. The blood from his face immediately drained away, turning him a ghost shade of white. Kryton had to hide his smile.

On the screen was a video of a man, wearing an orange jumpsuit and sitting in a chair, guarded by two large men holding automatic weapons and concealing their faces.

The jumpsuit started to speak.

"My name is Peter Wallis. I am a former NSA agent and I was involved in working with the Vice President in trying to assassinate President Jack Lang."

Kendrick's jaw hit the floor. He looked at the video. It showed Wallis holding a copy of that day's newspaper. It was the same version of the newspaper that Kryton had been looking at earlier in the lobby.

President Lang walked over and took the tablet away from Kendrick, handing it back to Dawn. He looked down at the pitiful sight in front of him.

"How do you think we deciphered all the information in that folder?" he said to Kendrick.

Kendrick looked defeated. He had not been expecting that.

"But…but they said he was dead," he mumbled.

"That was a little ruse from the good folks at CIA," said Lang, smiling satisfactorily.

"You recruited him into your plot based on your knowledge of his skills from when you ran the NSA. You conspired with him, through your nephew, to hatch a plan to assassinate me. You engaged with your Chinese links to fund, help organise and execute it all, including another attack in Taipei. When it went bad, you tried to destroy all the evidence and save your own arse."

Kendrick looked up at the President. He still couldn't believe that he had been caught.

"We offered Wallis reduced sentencing for helping to give you up. He was the one who deciphered the SD card recovered in Hong Kong, the card your Chinese friends were going to barter with to save their own arses. It was his code, after all, that was protecting it. And by reduced sentencing, I mean that we took the death penalty off of the table. He'll be joining your nephew in some very dark places for a very long time."

The Vice President sat back and sighed. His lip started to tremble.

"What about me?"

"Well, I'm not a lawyer. You were though, weren't you Ed! Our laws are pretty similar. You think the evidence will hold up in court?"

"Yes, it certainly will, Mister President," said the Prime Minister.

"Then I imagine you'll be going to some very dark places, too," said Lang.

The President returned to his desk and pressed a button on the intercom. Kryton watched as several FBI agents entered the room, as pre-arranged, and arrested the Vice President, right there in the Oval Office and over the official seal of the President of the United States.

A few moments later, the room had been cleared.

Lang stood by his desk, finishing his glass of whiskey. Director Dawn packed up the file. It was now evidence that would be used in the Vice President's trial, but it was still highly sensitive documents of national security.

The Prime Minister turned to Kryton, gesturing for them both to get up and give the President some space.

"We'll give you some room, Mister President."

Lang looked up, being pulled back into the room from his deep thoughts. The attempted assassination, as organised by the Vice President of all people, was a hard thing for him to have to come to terms with, both personally and professionally. His administration might not survive the scandal. He still had a country to run for the moment, though.

"No, we've got something we'd like to discuss with you...with you and Sergeant Kryton. Will you join us in the Situation Room?"

# 21

Jo adjusted her designer sunglasses as she walked along the lake, conducting her morning ritual of heading out from her office for a coffee, hoping to get some privacy before the lunch crowds descended on the trendy area in the nation's capital.

She walked into her favourite spot; a small café close to the water's edge. She smiled as she saw that her favourite seat was unoccupied. The fire was still going, even though it was starting to transition from winter into spring. There was only a handful of other customers in the café, quietly keeping to themselves.

She sat down, leaning into the familiar comfort and warmth of the seat that would allow her to keep her mind off of work for at least forty-five minutes. She took a cursory glance at the local newspaper sitting on the coffee table in front of her. The news had already segued back to domestic events. In this instance, the headlines talked about potential tax increases to fund increased government spending on national security.

She just rolled her eyes and sat back in her seat, closing them tightly.

An arm reached out from behind her, placing a cup down on the coffee table.

"Flat white, I assume?" said the kind voice.

Jo opened her eyes and started to turn her head.

"Oh, you guys must have seen me coming —"

She stopped talking as a man softly sat down in the seat adjacent to hers. He wore a dark peacoat over his V-neck shirt, jeans and dark brown leather boots. He leaned back into the seat and smiled.

"Zach!" she said, caught completely by surprise.

"Hey Jo," he replied.

She looked around the café, wondering what other surprises might be awaiting her.

"What are you doing here?" she asked once she had gathered her thoughts.

"Well, I promised you a coffee. So, here it is."

He leaned forward, looking closely at her.

"I'm sorry it took me so long."

She returned his gaze. A familiar feeling was rising in the pit of her stomach. She turned her head, trying unsuccessfully to conceal a girlish laugh. She composed herself and looked back at him. She noticed the few bruises, which were starting to fade.

"You look like you've been in the wars," she said.

He smiled and nodded his head.

"Yeah, it's umm…it's been an interesting week."

"The word around the office is that you and Jonas are some kind of heroes, saving the day and all that," she said teasingly.

She was happy that they were able to chat with ease like they had in the old days. She was so happy that he was alright.

"I've been trying to keep out of trouble. I'm not having much luck in that regard, though," he said.

He watched her as she took a sip of her coffee. She looked back at him. She had so many questions. She knew she probably wouldn't get the answers. Security being based on the principle of 'need-to-know' and all that.

She decided to try her luck anyway.

"Do we know why it was the Vice President? Why he did it?" she asked.

Kryton just shrugged his shoulders. It was a good question, but unfortunately not one he had the answer to.

"Who knows. Aren't all those things usually about having power?" he asked rhetorically.

She nodded.

"So, what now? Are you finished? Back to teaching cadets at RMC?"

Kryton tilted his head to his right, observing as the waitress opened the door to allow a small group of Chinese students inside. He looked back at her, inching slowly closer.

"Not just yet," he said.

"Not just yet?" she replied, looking at him curiously and finding herself also leaning forward into her seat.

He reached into his coat pocket, pulling out a plain white envelope and passing it to her. She cautiously opened it, pulling out the neatly

131

folded single page within. Her eyes widened as she quietly read the formal document.

She looked up at him.

He smiled softly and spoke.

"How would you like to help me make the world a safer place?"

Zach Kryton will be back…

Please feel free to follow us on social media and
provide recommendations and feedback!

## INSTAGRAM

### joshfrancis_red.diamond

## FACEBOOK

### joshfrancisbooks

INSTAGRAM

FACEBOOK

AMAZON

Please leave an honest review on Amazon. This helps to tailor better
content and allows for reader interaction.

Sign up to the readers group

# Biography

Josh Francis qualified as high school teacher before commissioning into the Royal Australian Navy as a junior officer soon after the September 11 attacks in the U.S. A desire to serve on warlike operations saw him resign his commission and enlist into the Australian Army. After qualifying as an infantryman and paratrooper, Josh deployed on peacekeeping operations in Timor-Leste conducting counter-militia operations.

After completing basic and specialist intelligence operations training, Josh completed multiple deployments to Afghanistan and Iraq, conducting duties in conventional and special operations, as well as training roles.

He is the author of the military themed personal development books *The Camouflage Series*, as well as the *Zach Kryton* series of books. His debut book is titled *Under the Pump*, a memoir about his youthful antics while working at a petrol station in his hometown of Adelaide.

www.ingramcontent.com/pod-product-compliance
Lightning Source LLC
Chambersburg PA
CBHW070338130626
46556CB00007B/2923